FROM THE
NANCY DREW FILES

THE CASE: Nancy investigates a series of attacks on the daughter of a rich Italian industrialist.

CONTACT: So far Gina Fiorella has faced arson, assault, and burglary. Kidnapping—or worse—could be next.

SUSPECTS: Jane Sellery—As Gina's rival for the National Honors Scholarship, she may have decided to put Gina out of the running . . . for good.

Nick Kessler—Gina fired him as her bodyguard and hired Ned as his replacement. He could be out to prove he's irreplaceable.

Paul Lampedusa—An old boyfriend of Gina's sister, he has a grudge against the whole Fiorella family.

COMPLICATIONS: Nancy knows she has to do the right thing—protect Gina—even if it means giving Gina a chance to steal Ned away.

Books in The Nancy Drew Files® Series

Available from ARCHWAY Paperbacks

The NANCY DREW Files™

110

HIDDEN MEANINGS

CAROLYN KEENE

AN ARCHWAY PAPERBACK
Published by POCKET BOOKS
New York   London   Toronto   Sydney   Tokyo   Singapore

AN ARCHWAY PAPERBACK *Original*

An Archway Paperback published by
POCKET BOOKS, a division of Simon & Schuster Inc.
1230 Avenue of the Americas, New York, NY 10020

Copyright © 1995 by Simon & Schuster Inc.
Produced by Mega-Books, Inc.

ISBN: 0-671-88201-5

First Archway Paperback printing August 1995

10 9 8 7 6 5 4 3 2 1

NANCY DREW, AN ARCHWAY PAPERBACK and colophon are registered trademarks of Simon & Schuster Inc.

THE NANCY DREW FILES is a trademark of Simon & Schuster Inc.

Cover art by Cliff Miller

Printed in the U.S.A.

IL 6+

HIDDEN
MEANINGS

Chapter

One

"Wow, who would ever have believed it—a truly awesome hotel here in River Heights!"

Staring up at the soaring lobby of the Atrium Hotel, Nancy Drew could only nod in agreement with the comment from her boyfriend, Ned Nickerson. Nancy and Ned were standing at the top of a black marble ramp just inside the front doors of the hotel. For months Nancy had noticed the tower of pink granite and dark glass rising on the edge of the college campus. But the new high-rise hotel had opened only the weekend before, and this was her first look inside.

Three glass-sided elevators glided up and down one side of the atrium. Guests inside could look down upon the lobby as they were whooshed smoothly to their floors. All guest room doors opened directly onto balcony walkways that overlooked the lobby twelve stories below.

An entire wall was made of glass—huge triangular panes angled to flood the atrium with sunlight. Delicate ficus trees, hanging plants, and banks of lush greenery had been planted all over the lobby. "It's almost like a giant greenhouse," Nancy remarked. "I guess all the fountains and reflecting pools keep it cool, even on hot days like today."

"I'll bet you could go whitewater rafting on that layout," Ned joked. He pointed to a pair of gleaming escalators leading to a mezzanine level, where a café had been set under the immense glass wall. A huge fountain there flowed into a steel water sculpture, which sent the water down into a long central pool in the lobby. A footbridge led over the pool. A series of cascades splashed down to another pool near the reception desk, on a level below the lobby.

"Nan, let's take the elevator to the top floor to get the whole view," Ned suggested, pulling on Nancy's arm.

"Okay—in a minute," Nancy said, tucking a strand of reddish blond hair into her ponytail. "First, I need to bring this bag to Bess." She swung the pink duffel bag she'd picked up from her friend Bess Marvin's house onto her shoulder. "She needs a change of clothes now that Mr. Ruxton has asked her to work at the banquet tonight."

Ned pointed to a chrome-framed sign on a nearby wall. "There's a schedule of all the events being held in the hotel today," he said. "Let's check it out."

Nancy and Ned walked over and studied the list. "This has to be it—'The Great Lakes High School Press Association,'" Nancy read aloud. "It says their registration area is in the Muskoka Lobby."

"It shouldn't be too hard for us to find the Muskoka Lobby," Ned said. "We'll just follow the crowd." He nodded toward a chattering swarm of high school students heading down a carpeted side corridor. Ned and Nancy trailed after the group.

On one side of the corridor was a row of boutiques. On the other, a pair of doors opened onto a carpeted reception area, used for seminars and conferences. As Nancy and Ned entered this area behind the students, Nancy spotted Bess sitting behind a registration table set up under a huge white banner with Welcome Great Lakes High School Press Association sewn across it in red block letters. Nancy waved, but the students crowding around the table completely occupied Bess's attention.

"Why is Bess working here?" Ned asked Nancy.

"This is a summer workshop for high school yearbook editors," Nancy explained. "It's being hosted this year by River Heights High, so the River Heights journalism teacher is in charge. He's also the yearbook advisor. Bess heard that he needed volunteers to help on opening day, so she signed up."

"I remember your telling me about the journalism teacher. He had long hair and tinted glasses," Ned said. "What was his name?"

"Mr. Ruxton," Nancy said. She pointed to the end of the registration table, where a man about thirty years old, dressed in a khaki jacket, was giving out registration packets. Nancy smiled, picturing how his gray eyes used to sparkle behind the pink-tinted lenses of his glasses. "Bess used to hang around the yearbook office, just to be near him," she said. "She always thought he was so cute."

"I never could keep track of all of Bess's crushes," Ned said with a grin.

Nancy gave Ned a playful dig in the ribs. "Come on—she wasn't *that* bad."

"Oh, yes, she was," Ned insisted. "I've always thought she was a terrible influence on you."

Nancy grinned. She knew that Ned was teasing her. Nancy and Bess Marvin had been friends nearly all their lives. Nancy depended on Bess and her cousin George Fayne for friendship and support. No one was more aware of that than Ned.

Nancy edged around the crowd to get closer to Bess. As she neared the table, a boy with a fade haircut reached the front of the line. Bess checked off his name on a long printout. Then she handed him a manila envelope.

"Your room key is in here, plus a list of the

4

seminars you signed up for," Bess told him. "You'll also find your name tag and conference schedule, as well as information about the contests."

The boy blinked in confusion. "Contests?"

"We have several competitions you can enter," Bess explained to the boy. "Feature writing, caption writing, headline writing, photography, layout, design—the works. Prizes will be announced at the final banquet Friday night."

As the boy stepped away from the table, Nancy waved to get Bess's attention. Bess glanced up and Nancy lifted the pink duffel bag over the students' heads. Bess nodded, holding up one finger to signal that she'd be with Nancy in a moment.

Ned came up behind Nancy. "Did she see you?" he asked her softly. Feeling his breath warm in her ear, Nancy leaned back against his broad chest and sighed contentedly.

With Ned away at Emerson College, they'd been apart for most of the year, and Nancy had missed him. Both of them had dated other people occasionally, but right now there was no one else in Nancy's life—and she had to admit that Ned looked more attractive than ever.

Just then Bess skirted around the table and met her friends. "How's it going?" Nancy asked, handing Bess the duffel bag.

"Oh, it's so exciting," Bess said. "These kids come from all over—Cleveland, St. Louis, some from Canada. They're all so keyed up, it's sort of contagious." She unzipped her bag and peeked inside. "Good—Mom remembered my hair dryer. I want to look great tonight. I'm working *very* closely with Gary. He treats me like a real adult now." She glanced back at the registration table just as Gary Ruxton crossed the lobby toward them. Bess looked suddenly nervous.

"Hello, Mr. Ruxton," Bess called out.

The teacher smiled. "Hello, Bess. And look who's here—Nancy Drew."

"I'm impressed that you remember me," Nancy said.

"Of course I'd remember an all-around good student like you, Nancy," Mr. Ruxton said. "And besides," he added with a chuckle, "your picture was in the yearbook on a dozen pages your senior year." Mr. Ruxton turned to Bess. "Taking a break?" he asked.

"Oh, no, Mr. Ruxton, not if you need me," Bess replied eagerly.

"Can you take my place for five minutes?" he asked. "Our keynote speaker for Friday night is due to arrive any minute, and—" He broke off, his gaze shifting to the conference area entrance. "There he is now. Excuse me."

"I'll introduce you later," Nancy said to Ned as the three friends turned to watch the teacher hurry to the doorway. Just inside stood a trim, broad-shouldered man in a perfectly cut blue suit. With his steel gray eyes, brown hair turning silver at the temples, and craggy good looks, he was instantly recognizable: Evan Sharpless, network TV reporter.

Even Nancy felt the impact of Sharpless's good looks. She glanced at Bess and saw her friend catch her breath. "Wow, he's good looking enough on television, but you just don't expect someone to be that handsome in person," Bess said with a sigh.

"That old guy? He must be nearly forty," Ned said disdainfully. Nancy smiled, amused by Ned's jealousy.

"Who cares?" Bess moaned.

"He's supposed to be an ace reporter," Nancy said, knowing her comment would needle Ned. "Didn't he win some big award recently?"

"He's won *loads* of awards," Bess claimed. "He just won the Hazelden Prize for his reporting from Afghanistan. And he has a new book out. I've seen stacks of them in all the bookstore windows. It's about how he goes all over the globe, chasing down big international stories. And he has that dreamy deep voice—" She lowered her voice. "'This is Evan Sharpless, reporting from Moscow,'" she said, imitating his on-screen sign-off.

Across the reception area, students clustered around the famous newsman. Some held out copies of his book, asking for his autograph. "I wonder if Mr. Ruxton could introduce me to him," Bess said.

"You mean Gary?" Ned asked Bess. Nancy

elbowed Ned to stop teasing, but Bess hadn't noticed.

"Bess, I think you were supposed to cover the registration table," Nancy reminded her gently.

Bess looked over at the lines of students. "Oops—sorry. I'd better go," she said. "Well, see you guys later." She hurried back to her post.

As Nancy stood watching Evan Sharpless, Ned took her by the elbow. "Okay, mission accomplished," he said impatiently. "Let's head out. I want to try those elevators." Nancy nodded, and she and Ned trailed after the crowd following the famous newscaster back to the main lobby.

Reaching the lobby, they saw Mr. Sharpless shake hands with Gary Ruxton, wave goodbye to the students, and step onto the escalator leading up to the mezzanine. As the reporter glided upward, Nancy saw one of the students pointing a camera with a jutting telephoto lens at him. Pushing back her thick, curly light brown hair, the tall girl crouched for a better angle. Nancy admired her instinct for a dramatic shot.

Nancy saw the newscaster step off onto the mezzanine. "Looks like he's meeting someone there," she commented to Ned. Another man who had been leaning over the railing watching the lobby straightened up and walked over to Evan Sharpless.

Ned shrugged. "Maybe another adoring news fan."

Crossing over to the far side of the lobby, Nancy and Ned waited near the elevators, surrounded by chattering high-schoolers. Three girls were standing on the footbridge that arched over the central pool, posing for a snapshot. Nancy noticed that the tall girl taking the picture was the same one who'd just been shooting pictures of Evan Sharpless.

As her friends mugged for the camera, the girl climbed up on the marble ledge around the pool to focus her shot. As she leaned over the water, she took the picture. Then another girl ran over and took the camera, so that the tall girl could get in the next picture.

Nancy turned to study Ned's face. "You look a little distracted, Nickerson," she said, gently prodding his shoe with the toe of her sneaker. "Too many pretty high school girls to look at?"

Ned flushed slightly as he turned back to her. "You know I have eyes for no one but you, Drew," he said good-humoredly, though it was clear to Nancy that he *had* been looking. "Anyway, it isn't that. I was thinking that I wish I hadn't agreed to end my job so early. I didn't save as much money as I should have. I don't know where it all went."

Nancy tensed. As a detective, she couldn't resist a juicy case, and a mystery had recently taken her away from River Heights. What had Ned been up to while she was away? she wondered.

"On the other hand," Ned went on in a brighter voice, "it *is* nice to have a little free time before I go back to Emerson."

"Well, maybe we can go away somewhere before the summer's over," Nancy suggested. She slipped a hand in the crook of his elbow and gave him a flirtatious tug. Ned met her eyes for a moment, and a wave of emotion seemed to rock them both.

But just then they heard a hollow rumble, a splash, and a scream. Nancy leapt up onto a chrome planter near the elevator bank to see what was the matter.

The dark-haired girl who'd taken the camera had tumbled into the pool. Her arms and legs flailing, she choked and sputtered wildly.

Suddenly the girl's head slid under the surface of the water. Nancy watched in horror as the girl was pulled along by the current—head first toward the cascade!

Chapter

Two

Acting on instinct, Ned vaulted up onto the black marble ledge beside the reflecting pool. "Get Mr. Ruxton!" he yelled over his shoulder to Nancy. Then he flung himself into the pool.

Knowing Ned would rescue the girl, Nancy peered over the heads of the crowd that had rushed over to the water. Mr. Ruxton had been here a few minutes earlier, saying goodbye to Evan Sharpless. Had he already gone back to the registration lobby?

Nancy leapt down from the planter box, then raced up the side corridor and into the Muskoka Lobby. Spotting Gary Ruxton near the picture window with another teacher, she called to him from the doorway. "Mr. Ruxton—a student fell into the pool!"

Mr. Ruxton moved quickly. "Swimming pool or lobby pool?" he asked, sprinting for the door.

"Lobby pool," Nancy replied. She spun around and ran beside him toward the lobby. "Ned jumped in to try to get her before she went down the waterfall."

They charged up the corridor and into the main lobby. Nancy spotted an overturned luggage trolley at the foot of the black marble ramp running down from the front doors. A bellman in a red uniform was picking up the pile of suitcases that had fallen off it. Stepping over the bags, Nancy sized up what had happened. The trolley must have rolled out of control down the ramp and crashed into the ledge right by the footbridge, knocking the girl into the water.

Nancy and Mr. Ruxton reached the girl, who was sitting on the marble ledge, her friends gathered around her. Ned, soaking wet, was climbing out of the pool.

"What happened?" Gary Ruxton demanded. The crowd parted, and Nancy looked at the girl. Even with water streaming from her long dark hair and clothes, Nancy could tell the girl was strikingly beautiful. Her figure was petite but shapely and her delicate, olive-skinned face had a full mouth and huge dark eyes.

The girl drew a deep breath. "I was on the ledge, trying to get everyone in the picture," she told Mr. Ruxton. "Then I heard a loud noise behind me. I looked around and saw this big luggage cart rolling down the ramp. It came right at me!"

She shivered and went on. "I think a garment bag swinging from the rail on top knocked me into the pool," she added. "The current—it started to pull me down. And then . . . someone saved me." She twisted around, and her dark eyes stared up into Ned's. Nancy felt her stomach flip over with jealousy.

"Can someone go get a towel?" piped the tall, curly-haired girl, standing by the wet girl's side.

"Uh, of course," Mr. Ruxton responded, looking around. "At the swimming pool—level three—"

Bess materialized out of the crowd. Nancy guessed that she'd been too curious to stay behind, once she'd seen Nancy run in to get Mr. Ruxton. "I'll go," Bess said, and hurried away.

Mr. Ruxton knelt beside the dark-haired girl. "What's your name?" he asked her.

"G-Gina. Gina Fiorella." She forced out the words between chattering teeth.

Nancy noticed the teacher rock back on his heels and let out a slight gasp. "From Lloyd Hall, right?" he asked. "Near Chicago?" Gina nodded.

"She's editor of our yearbook, the *Cameo*," her friend added.

Mr. Ruxton twisted around to look at the curly-haired girl. "And you are—?" he inquired.

The girl blushed shyly. "I'm her coeditor, Sally Harvey," she replied. "And her roommate."

"Oh, yes—Lloyd Hall is a boarding school, right?" Mr. Ruxton said. Gina nodded.

Just then Sally drew a startled breath. "Gina—the camera! You had it in your hand when you fell—"

Gina waved a careless hand toward the pool. "Oh, it's in there somewhere," she said.

Sally jumped up onto the marble ledge and began to look for the camera at the bottom of the pool.

As Ned climbed up beside Sally to help her look, Gina reached up and tugged on his wet T-shirt. "Hey—you're my knight in shining armor," she murmured. Her voice had gotten low and husky. Ned, looking down, flashed her a broad grin. Nancy, wedged in the crowd behind Gary Ruxton, did a slow burn.

Just then Bess hurried up with an armload of fresh white towels and handed them to Gina. The girl pulled two off the top of the pile and handed them up to Ned. "Come down and dry off," she commanded, with a mischievous look from under thick dark lashes. Ned, with another grin, obeyed.

A woman in a business suit ran over the bridge. "Mr. Ruxton, I just heard about the accident. Is everything under control?"

"I think so, Ms. Peabody," Mr. Ruxton answered. "Right, Ms. Fiorella?"

"I'm fine," Gina replied.

"Ms. Fiorella?" The woman seemed to react to the girl's name in the same way Mr. Ruxton had—with a tinge of awe. She leaned over solicitously. "I'm Maureen Peabody, the general manager of the Atrium Hotel," she said, introducing herself. "You have towels, I see. Let me get you a hot drink. Can I help you to your room?"

"What's going on?" a male voice boomed. A tall, muscular man in a dark sweater and jeans lumbered up, stuffing the last of a sandwich into his mouth. Gina turned toward him with narrowed eyes.

"You're late, Nick," she snapped.

"I told you I was getting lunch," he protested.

"You were hired to protect me," she said. "You were supposed to be back at two. I almost drowned! If it hadn't been for this guy—" She reached up to grab Ned's hand.

Ned looked over at Nancy and gave a helpless shrug. Nancy lifted her chin. Ned didn't pull his hand away, she noted. Her face set in cool indifference, Nancy turned to Bess. "Let's check out that luggage trolley," she murmured.

Nancy and Bess slipped away through the dispersing crowd and wandered over to the trolley. The two girls stood nearby as the bellman, whose name tag read Ralph Winkler, reloaded the luggage trolley. Holding onto the brass top rail, Ralph fidgeted as a thickset middle-aged man in a polyester sport jacket spoke to him.

"But, Mr. Wasilick!" Ralph protested. "I *had* to leave the trolley unattended. A guest in a wheelchair asked me to help him down the ramp. That's what we were told in training—guests come first."

"Well, that trolley didn't take off by itself," Mr. Wasilick insisted.

"I left it six feet from the top of the ramp. Someone must have pushed it," Ralph declared. "The next thing I knew, I heard it rolling. I turned around and it was already down by the pool."

"Well, that's no excuse," Mr. Wasilick said. "You know who that girl down there is?" Nancy perked up, listening. "Her daddy is none other than Lorenzo Fiorella, one of the richest men in Italy," Mr. Wasilick said. "I spent three hours yesterday with that bodyguard of hers, just to prove that my security setup here is A-OK. And then this happens. We could get hit with a whale of a lawsuit."

Ralph stood limply beside the trolley as the security chief strode away. At that moment Bess piped up. "That ramp is awfully slick. I nearly slipped on it myself this morning. They ought to put some no-skid strips on it, like in bathtubs."

Ralph brightened immediately. "I *told* them it was dangerous," he said. "Architects design these dramatic spaces without thinking about how folks in wheelchairs will get around. The incline is a killer, and it ends two feet from the pool! They should redesign it."

"Maybe they will now," Bess said, trying to reassure him.

Ralph leaned eagerly toward Bess. "Are you a guest at the hotel?" he asked.

"Well, no—I'm just working here," she said. "At the workshop registration desk—"

"Great!" Ralph said. "You see, we have a policy against asking guests for dates. But since you're not a guest—will you have dinner with me tonight?"

Bess's face turned beet red, and Nancy quickly understood why. Gary Ruxton was walking past. He must have heard the bellman asking Bess out.

Embarrassed, Bess stammered, "Uh . . . uh . . . not tonight—I have to work at the banquet. Gotta run!" With that, Bess scooted off toward the Muskoka Lobby. Nancy silently ducked away, too, leaving Ralph alone with his trolley.

Heading back toward the lobby pool, Nancy passed Gina Fiorella, swaddled in towels, being helped by her roommate to the elevators. Ned stood at the end of the bridge, rubbing his hair dry with a towel. As Nancy joined him, Gary Ruxton hurried over. Nancy introduced Mr. Ruxton to Ned. "Ned, Nancy, thanks so much for your help," Mr. Ruxton said. "What can I do to repay you? Can you join us here tonight for our kick-off banquet?"

"Sure, thanks," Nancy replied eagerly.

"Riverview Ballroom, seven o'clock," the teacher announced, and he dashed away with a parting wave.

"Okay with you?" Nancy asked Ned gingerly. Something about his mood troubled her.

"Well, actually—I have to work tonight," Ned said, not quite meeting her eyes.

Nancy frowned. "I thought you said your summer job was over," she said, puzzled.

Ned stared down at his sopping shoes. "This is something else," he muttered. "That girl—the one who fell in the pool—just offered me a job."

Nancy felt stunned. "A job?" she repeated.

"She wants me to be her new bodyguard," Ned explained, finally looking up at her. "She fired that other guy and asked me to replace him. I have to go home now to pack. She wants me to stay here in the hotel, in the room right next to hers." He threw her a pleading glance. "It's just until the conference ends, and it pays really well. I could sure use the money, Nan."

Nancy willed her voice to be steady as she turned and began to walk up the ramp to the front doors. "But you aren't a trained body-guard," she said evenly.

"So, what do I have to know?" Ned complained, following her. "All I have to do is trail her around, guard her room at night, that kind of thing. Just from helping you on cases, I probably know more than that Nick guy did."

Great, thought Nancy. *My* cases have trained Ned for a job hanging around *her*.

Entering the Riverview Ballroom at six forty-five that evening, Nancy drifted through the crowd alone. She scanned the crowd, trying to spot Gina and Ned. Her heart sank when she couldn't find them anywhere.

She admitted to herself that seeing them together would bother her a lot. But *not* seeing them made her feel even worse. All she could think was that they must be somewhere else—together.

Nearby, Evan Sharpless was chatting with a group of students. It's nice of him to spend so much time with them, Nancy mused. For a celebrity, he didn't seem at all snobby.

Then she saw Sally Harvey standing with some friends, camera in hand. Nancy stepped over to her. "I see you got your camera back," she commented.

Sally gave Nancy a blank look, clearly not recognizing her. With so many people crowded around Gina in the lobby that afternoon, Sally probably hadn't noticed their faces, Nancy realized.

"Oh, yes—it went down the cascades and ended up in the pool at the bottom," Sally replied.

"Does it still work?" Nancy asked.

Sally nodded, then grinned. Nancy saw that even if Sally didn't know her, she was still ready to be friendly. "Luckily, this is a waterproof camera," Sally explained. "My friend Gina and I just came from Florida, where we were doing some scuba diving. It was my birthday, so she bought me this camera for underwater photography."

Then Sally's gaze was drawn to the ballroom entrance. Nancy followed her eyes and saw Gina enter the ballroom. Ned was nowhere in sight.

Gina, dressed in a chic blue minidress, made a beeline for Gary Ruxton. Her imperious manner and her dazzling looks cast a hush over the crowd. "Well, Mr. Ruxton," she called out in a loud voice. "Almost getting drowned was bad enough. But now this!"

"What are you talking about, Gina?" Mr. Ruxton asked, perplexed. People edged closer to catch her answer.

With a fiery glare, she announced dramatically, "Somebody just broke into my hotel room!"

Chapter

Three

NANCY HEARD Sally Harvey gasp. Then she noticed the blood draining from Gary Ruxton's face. "Your room was broken into?" he repeated. "I'd better call hotel security," he said. "Don't go back to the room alone. I'll go with you."

Before he left, Mr. Ruxton gave the students who had been listening a reassuring smile. "Nothing to worry about, I'm sure," he announced. "Go ahead and sit down to dinner, everyone. We'll take care of this problem." He took Gina by the arm and led her away before she could say anything. Sally hurried to follow them out the door.

Nancy slipped quietly through the crowd and out the ballroom door. Gina and Sally were standing near the escalator leading down to the Muskoka Lobby. Gary Ruxton was at a nearby

21

phone, calling security. Nancy walked up and waited for him to finish his call.

Hanging up, Mr. Ruxton looked at her squarely. "Nancy, I know your reputation as a detective," he said. "Maybe you can get to the bottom of this."

"I'd be happy to help," Nancy told him.

Gina's dark eyes widened. "This girl is a detective?" she asked skeptically.

"Yes—and a very good one, too," Mr. Ruxton declared. "Nancy, this is Gina Fiorella—Gina, Nancy Drew. Now, Gina, what's your room number?"

"We're in 707," Gina said. "But surely we don't need a detective!" She tagged after the teacher as he headed for the elevators. "I have my own bodyguard."

"Nancy happens to be here tonight as my guest," Mr. Ruxton explained. "It won't hurt to get her advice."

An elevator arrived, and Nancy, Gina, and Mr. Ruxton stepped inside. Once upstairs, Gina led the way to her room. Mr. Wasilick, the hotel security chief, was standing outside the open door. Beside him, Ned leaned over the balcony railing, looking down into the atrium. Nancy flashed Ned a quick look, silently warning him not to let on that they knew each other. He nodded and looked away quickly. Nancy hoped that Mr. Ruxton wouldn't unintentionally blow their cover.

Through the open door, Nancy could see that

the room was a shambles. Drawers were pulled out, and their contents were spread around. Closet doors stood open, and suitcase lids gaped wide.

"Sally had already gone down to the banquet," Gina explained. "I'd just stopped by Ned's room, to see if he was settled in okay. He's next door, in 709." Her eyes danced as she threw Ned a dazzling smile. "Anyway, he and I passed by my room on our way to the elevator, and we saw this." She gestured toward the mess.

"We didn't go inside," Ned added. "I thought it was best to alert the authorities right away. I sent Gina down and I stayed here, watching the room."

"So you don't even know if anything's missing?" Mr. Wasilick asked. Gina shook her head. He sighed. "Let's go assess the damage," he said.

Mr. Wasilick, Gina, and Sally entered the room, with Nancy and Mr. Ruxton close behind them. Ned stayed just inside the door.

Gina walked straight to a small leather case on a shelf in the closet. Quickly working the combination lock, she lifted the lid. "Well, thank goodness my jewelry's all here," she announced.

"My cameras are here, too," Sally added, looking inside a black canvas case sitting near the TV set.

Maureen Peabody appeared in the doorway. "Oh, Ms. Fiorella, I can't believe this has happened!" she exclaimed.

Gina wheeled around to face the hotel manager. She turned on a hundred-watt smile. "Thanks for your concern," she said sweetly. "Luckily, our valuables weren't taken. They were in locked cases. Maybe our thief was an amateur who couldn't break them open."

"But that jewel case is fairly small," Nancy spoke up. "Why didn't the thief just take it away?"

Gina looked annoyed at Nancy's comment.

Mr. Wasilick hooked his fingers in his belt. "I doubt if the motive was robbery at all," he said. "Maybe someone wanted to hurt you, Ms. Fiorella. You weren't here, so whoever it was messed things up to scare you."

Nancy noticed Sally Harvey flinch. Gina, however, tossed her thick, wavy dark hair. "Well, things like this don't scare me," she replied.

While Gina and Sally continued to check their belongings, Maureen Peabody and Gary Ruxton went out into the hallway to confer. A moment or two later, Ms. Peabody signaled to Nancy to join them.

"Mr. Ruxton tells me that you're an experienced detective," the general manager said. "He has great faith in you. I was wondering if you could hang around the workshop and keep your eye on things. This break-in may be nothing, but it makes me nervous—especially after what happened to Gina this afternoon."

Nancy nodded, thinking to herself that this setup would also allow her to keep an eye on Ned.

"I understand that Gina's father is very wealthy," she began.

"Enormously wealthy—and he has strong political connections in Italy," Ms. Peabody said. "I've heard he has more than his share of enemies. Some of them might try to hurt him through his daughter."

Nancy felt a tug of excitement at the prospect of such an intriguing case. So this case would be more than just protecting a spoiled rich girl, she thought.

"You're young—you can blend into the crowd at the conference better than Stan Wasilick can," Ms. Peabody said. "In a hotel, there are always crowds of people. The more eyes we have, the better."

"In that case," Nancy said, "I have two friends who could help—Bess Marvin and George Fayne. Bess is already working at the conference, as a matter of fact. While I'm watching Gina at the workshop, they could easily work behind the scenes. After all, I doubt a workshop student is our culprit."

Ms. Peabody looked interested. "I can arrange for them to go undercover," she said. "Bess could be a server at the workshop meals, and I could get George in as a pool lifeguard. Can he swim?"

Nancy hid a grin. "Yes, *she* can," she said, correcting the general manager. "George is a girl."

"I'm very sorry!" Ms. Peabody said, looking embarrassed.

"Don't worry. With that name, it's an easy mistake," Nancy assured her. "But I just thought of one problem—Bess worked at the registration table today. Won't the workshop participants recognize her?"

"They probably thought she was a hotel employee," Ms. Peabody said. "The truth is, hotel guests don't usually notice employees' faces. I'll speak to the front desk and get you a room right down the hall, if possible," Ms. Peabody said.

Nancy nodded. "George and Bess could share the room, too," she suggested. "If they're careful about coming and going, they won't blow their covers."

Just then Stan Wasilick came to the door. "No evidence in there," he said. "No sign of a break-in at the door. I'll bet our thief used a keycard."

"Keycard?" Nancy asked.

The security chief shot her a suspicious look. "Who are you, anyway?" he demanded.

Ms. Peabody cleared her throat. "Stan, this is Nancy Drew. She's a detective, and I've asked her to help us on this case." Mr. Wasilick raised his eyebrows. Nancy could tell he was skeptical of her.

"Well, miss, this hotel uses keycards, not metal keys," he explained, pulling from his pocket a rectangle of thin gray plastic that looked very much like a credit card. "A guest just slides this card into this slot to open the lock." He pointed out a three-inch-wide slot in the metal plate below the room's doorknob.

"For security purposes, the cards don't have room numbers on them," Mr. Wasilick added. "Those two girls say they didn't lose their cards, but I'll bet one of them put hers down for a second and someone borrowed it—someone who *knew* their room number."

"How does the housekeeping staff gain access to a room if the guest is out?" Nancy asked.

The security chief looked surprised. "Good question. Uh, they have a passkey," he said. "See that little lock below the keycard slot? That's for the passkey."

"So anyone from the housekeeping staff could have gotten in," Nancy suggested.

"Only the maids assigned to this floor," he said hastily. "Each floor has a different passkey. And I'm going right now to question the maid on duty."

Nancy hid a smile as he hurried away. She could tell he hadn't thought of that angle.

Nancy asked the general manager if she could interview the two girls. Ms. Peabody agreed, and Nancy went back into their room. Ned, who had been waiting near the door, stepped outside as she came in. Nancy was careful not to meet his eyes.

Gina and Sally were still straightening up, but they gladly answered Nancy's questions. Sally said she'd left the room at six to meet friends downstairs. Gina repeated her story about finding the room a mess.

"Any idea who might've done this?" Nancy asked, leaning against a dresser.

"One of my dad's enemies." Gina sighed as she flopped into a chair. "Or one of my own enemies."

Nancy raised her eyebrows. "Your enemies?"

Gina looked bored. "My rivals, of course," she said. "There's Jane Sellery, editor of the *Folio* at Brookfield Academy. It's a dreadful yearbook, but for some reason she thinks we're rivals. She's at the workshop—I saw her this afternoon, in the lobby. When that trolley rolled down the ramp, she was standing right behind it!"

"Are you sure about that?" Nancy asked, straightening up.

Gina nodded. "Jane's hard to miss. She's nearly six feet tall, and her hair is red as a carrot."

"What could she gain by raiding your room, or by knocking you into the pool?" Nancy asked.

"We're both National Scholars finalists," Gina said loftily. "They accept only one boy and one girl from each state. Maybe she thinks she'll win if she knocks me out of the running."

"Oh, Gina, I don't believe that," Sally said. "Jane's competitive, but she's not evil. Anyway, you're sure to win. Your grades are just as good as hers, and your extracurricular record is much stronger. Plus, your yearbook is better."

"*Our* yearbook," Gina corrected her, flashing her friend a warm smile.

"Well, I'll look into this angle," Nancy promised. "Her name is Jane Sellery?"

"Yes. Sounds like the vegetable, 'celery,' but it starts with an *S,*" Gina told Nancy.

Just then, angry male voices could be heard outside the door. Gina and Sally traded questioning glances. "We'd better see what's going on," Nancy said. The three girls moved to the door and listened.

"Replace me? You amateur!" one voice sputtered.

Gina gaped. "That's Nick Kessler, my old bodyguard," she whispered.

Nancy recognized Ned's voice. "I just plan to stay alert and do what I can to help Gina," he said.

"Ms. Fiorella to you!" Nick growled. "And you'll learn she's not so easy to guard. When she wants you around, she's all smiles and big eyes. But if she wants her freedom, she'll disappear out from under your nose."

"Hey, buddy, it's not my fault you messed up on the job," Ned said. Then the girls heard a thud against the door and Ned yelled, "Hey!" Nancy guessed Nick had shoved Ned.

"You just watch your step, lover boy," Nick shouted, his voice fading down the hallway. "If anything happens to her, you'll answer to me!"

There was silence in the hallway. Nancy squinted through the peephole and saw Ned leaning against the wall, his arms tightly folded and his jaw jutting out angrily. Knowing Ned's temper, Nancy realized he needed time to cool down.

Gina strolled away from the door, tossing her head haughtily. "Men!" she joked. "I think Ned could use a little cheering up. Let's take him to dinner, Sal—I'm starved."

Nancy's own stomach growled at the thought of dinner. "If you don't mind, I'd like to take a look around the room," she said.

Gina shrugged. "Okay with me. My bodyguard will be with us—just pull the door shut when you leave." Picking up her tiny designer leather purse, she grabbed Sally's arm and breezed out the door.

Stifling her resentment, Nancy began to inspect the room, starting with the door and windows. She examined the floor of the closet, and checked the locks on the suitcases. She couldn't help but note that Gina had three matching suitcases in expensive olive green leather, compared to Sally's one red canvas satchel and black camera carryall.

Nancy dropped to her knees to inspect the carpet. Stan Wasilick had found no clues, but Nancy hoped to find something, if she hunted hard enough.

Nearing the bed, she bent down to look underneath. A slim white object, about five inches long, gleamed in the shadows. Nancy pulled it out.

It was a ballpoint pen with a green crest printed on the side. Nancy looked closer.

The crest of Brookfield Academy—Jane Sellery's school!

Chapter
Four

SPRINGING TO HER FEET, Nancy slipped the Brookfield Academy pen into her pocket. Had Jane Sellery dropped it while breaking into Gina's room? she wondered. She decided to find Sellery and question her.

Nancy swiftly finished her inspection and headed down to the Muskoka Lobby. There, she found Bess sitting alone in the deserted registration area, looking bored. Some fried chicken and cold french fries lay on a plate before her. Bess perked up when she saw Nancy. "What's going on?" she asked.

Nancy pulled a chair close to the table and told Bess the whole story—about the break-in, Gina's accusation against Jane Sellery, and Nancy's finding the Brookfield pen. "I thought you and George could go undercover and help me," Nancy added.

Bess's eyes sparkled. "You bet!" she agreed. "And George has nothing going on this week— the tennis clinic where she was teaching has ended for the summer. I'll give her a call and ask her to come over right away. She can stop by our houses to pick up some clothes for us."

"Good," Nancy said. "Meanwhile, I'd like to question Jane, before I tell Gina I found this pen. Gina's having dinner now, with her roommate and Ned."

"With Ned?" Bess almost shrieked. "Are you nuts? Nancy, if I were you, I wouldn't let her within ten feet of my boyfriend."

Nancy squirmed in her chair. "Believe me, I don't like this setup either," she admitted. "But I forget to tell you that part—Gina fired her old bodyguard and hired Ned. Just until the conference is over."

"What!" Bess exclaimed. "How dare she? Well, George and I will help keep an eye on him, don't you worry. Anyway, let me look up Jane Sellery's room number for you." She turned to glance over the table top. Then she frowned. "Where's the registration list? It was here this evening, before I went up to the banquet to get my dinner."

"Maybe Mr. Ruxton took it," Nancy suggested.

"No, he told me it had to stay at the table," Bess insisted, panic rising in her voice. "This is the master list, where we checked off the names of the participants as they arrived. If I've lost it, he'll think I'm an idiot."

The two girls began to hunt for the computer printout. They looked through the cardboard cartons of extra registration packets. Then Nancy went around the table, shaking the skirt of the long light-blue cloth draped around it. At a back corner, she found the list on the floor under the table.

"Whew!" Bess exclaimed. "Someone must have knocked it onto the floor."

"Maybe," Nancy said grimly. "Or whoever broke into Gina's room took it to get her room number."

With a sigh, Bess scanned the list. "'Jane Sellery, Room 607,'" she read.

"Really," Nancy remarked. "That's right below Gina's room—she's in 707."

Bess knit her eyebrows. "It might be a coincidence," she declared. "All the girls are on floors six and seven, and all the boys are on eight and nine, but otherwise the room assignments were random."

"Okay, so it may not be significant," Nancy said. "Anyway, you go call George. See if she can meet us in the lobby in an hour."

"Got it," Bess said, moving toward a nearby phone.

Nancy said goodbye, then headed for the lobby elevators. She took one up to the sixth floor. Stepping out, she walked down the hall to Room

607 and knocked on the door. There was no answer. As she raised her knuckles to rap again, a gruff voice behind her asked, "Looking for someone?"

Nancy whirled to see a tall girl in a blue cotton dress. Her shoulder-length hair was carrot red. "Jane Sellery?" Nancy asked.

The girl narrowed her eyes. "That's me," she answered. "What did you want?"

"Um, I was just up in Gina Fiorella's room," Nancy said, improvising, "and I found this." She held up the pen. "I thought it might belong to you."

Jane looked at the pen but didn't take it. "My roommate, Karen, and I both have lots of Brookfield pens," she said. "But this can't be mine—I haven't been in *her* room." Her mouth twisted. "Everyone has those pens. Our school gives out tons of them."

"Just asking," Nancy said brightly. "Are you coming back from the banquet?"

"The banquet ended half an hour ago," Jane said. "I went to the pool. I always take a swim after dinner."

Nancy weighed this story. Jane's hair wasn't even wet, and she was fully dressed, with no towel or wet bathing suit in her hand. Had she really been swimming?

"Nice pool?" Nancy asked, hoping to sound friendly. Jane merely shrugged. Nancy pushed on. "Gina ought to check it out. She sure went swimming in the wrong pool this afternoon!"

Jane smirked. "Served her right," she muttered.

"You were there? You saw the accident?" Nancy asked in a gossipy-sounding voice. "I only heard about it later."

"I was just coming in the front door when I heard this splash," Jane said. "Then I saw Gina climb out of the pool. She was *soaked*. I don't know how it happened—maybe somebody had just had enough of her princessy ways." Jane started to chuckle, then stopped. "Are you a friend of hers?"

"No way," Nancy said heartily. "Say, did you hear her room got broken into?"

Jane stifled a smug smile. "Yeah, I heard that. Did all her stuff get ripped off?"

"No, nothing was stolen," Nancy said. "She has that big suite on the fifth floor, you know." Nancy watched closely to see if Jane noticed she had given her the wrong information.

Jane snorted. "Like I said, princess all the way," she remarked. "She couldn't stay in a regular room like the rest of us. Well, don't look at me—I haven't been on the fifth floor at all."

After saying good night, Nancy returned to the elevators. Back to square one, she thought while she waited. Jane clearly didn't like Gina, but she didn't seem to know anything about the break-in. When the elevator came, Nancy decided to return to the seventh floor to look around some more.

After getting off on seven, Nancy walked down

the hall, and noticed that Ned wasn't outside Gina's room. She bit her lip, thinking that Ned and Gina were probably still having dinner. Just then, Nancy saw a short, dark-haired girl in a gray cotton uniform poke her head out of a doorway. The girl, who was about Nancy's age, looked upset.

Nancy walked up. "Hi," she said, reading the plastic name tag on her uniform, which said Rosita Ortiz. "Can I talk with you, Rosita?"

Rosita quivered. "Are you the girl in Room 707?" she asked softly. "Because I've talked to Mr. Wasilick already. I told him I did not see anything. I was at the other end of the hall."

Nancy laid a hand gently on Rosita's arm. "I'm a friend of the girl in 707," she said. "And we just wondered how the thief got in."

Rosita's dark eyes filled with tears. "I've had my key with me the whole time," she said. "Please, I do not want to lose my job. I came to America six months ago from Peru and finally found a job. I've worked one week, and now this happens."

"You won't get fired," Nancy said soothingly. "I just need help. You know the hotel better than I do. Can you show me around?"

Brushing away her tears, Rosita led Nancy along the corridor to three locked white metal doors that looked almost invisible against the white walls. Inside were large supply closets, with shelves of bed linens, towels, wrapped bars of soap, and other items for the guest rooms, as well as huge canvas hampers filled with dirty sheets and towels.

Rosita took one of the hampers, which was mounted on wheels, and rolled it down the corridor. Near the end, she turned away from the atrium and through a pair of steel doors. Compared to the soft carpet, brass light fixtures, and artwork in the guest area, the back corridor was stark, with bare white walls, fluorescent lights, and a gray linoleum floor, Nancy noticed.

The service corridor ended at a large elevator. Rosita pushed the button, and the doors opened. She rolled the hamper inside. Another staff member, a man in a green coverall, stood next to a plastic bin of garbage.

"I guess I'll leave you here," Nancy said, wrinkling her nose at the stench. "If you see anything strange, will you be sure to tell me?"

Rosita smiled and nodded as the doors shut.

Nancy made her way back to the guest hallway. Looking down to the door of 707, she saw with a sinking heart that Ned *still* wasn't there. With a sigh, she headed down to the lobby to find Bess and George and to see about their room.

The next morning Nancy slept late. When she finally woke up, she dressed quickly and went down to the Muskoka Lobby. Once again it was buzzing with activity. Wearing a short red linen skirt and white cotton sweater, Nancy hoped to blend in with the students. Across the lobby she saw Bess at a buffet table, wearing a server's white blouse, black pants, and black bow tie. Pitchers of juice and platters of muffins covered the table, which had been set up for students who had slept late and missed the more elaborate breakfast earlier.

Waving to Bess, Nancy began to mingle with the students. She couldn't see Gina, but she did spot Sally's curly-haired head above the crowd as Sally stepped onto an escalator. Nancy followed her up to the next floor, where several oak-paneled doors and two corridors were visible from the red-carpeted landing.

Each door held a sign indicating which workshop was meeting inside. Nancy followed Sally into a room on the end of one corridor. The sign on the door said Advanced Photography Seminar.

Inside, a dozen students stood around what looked like a private dining room, waiting for the seminar to begin. Seeing Jane Sellery across the room, Nancy waved to her. Then she noticed a door ajar at the far end of the room. She went over and popped her head in. It was a windowless kitchenette that had been turned into a darkroom.

Strips of film hung to dry from clotheslines strung across the tiny darkroom, and next to the sink were pans of liquid developer. Sally was just reaching up to unclip some film from the line.

"Hi, Nancy," she said, greeting her. "The roll I shot yesterday is ready. Want to see?"

"Sure," Nancy said. She followed Sally back out to the main room. Sally laid the film down on a metal box that had a frosted glass top and a light below.

"These are just negatives, of course," Sally said, peering at the film. "I haven't printed anything yet. But I think I got some really good shots of Evan Sharpless on that escalator."

Nancy bent over the light box to examine the tiny images, each one less than an inch square. She could just make out a man's shape and the upward slant of an escalator. In each shot, the image changed slightly. The figure moved up the escalator, then onto the mezzanine, with its picture window behind. Sharpless was joined by a shorter figure, wearing baggy pants and with a bushy white beard. Then Nancy remembered that this was a reverse image—in the printed photo, the beard would be dark. She remembered the man she'd seen meeting Sharpless on the mezzanine. She figured he must be a friend of the newsman.

Just then Nancy heard a buzz in the room. She turned and saw Gina stroll in, in a dressy black pants outfit that bared her midriff. Nancy also spied Ned, hanging back by the doorway.

"Gina, look at these cool shots I took of Evan Sharpless," Sally said eagerly.

Gina leaned over the light table. "Sharpless?" she scoffed. "I don't know why everyone is fawning over him here. He may look good on the TV screen, but I wouldn't call him a reporter."

"What do you mean?" Sally argued. "He won the Hazelden Prize." She looked hurt, but Gina didn't seem to notice.

"Well, he must have paid off the judges," Gina said with a dismissive wave.

"Pay off the judges? That sounds more like your style, Gina," Jane Sellery said, speaking up from behind.

Whirling around, Gina narrowed her eyes. "I don't need to pay judges to win, Jane," she said. "Sally and I are creating a yearbook theme display that will amaze everyone. We'll win the top award, fair and square!" With that, she swept out of the room.

Jane chuckled. Sally looked away, embarrassed. "I'd better go," Nancy murmured, deciding to keep her eye on Ned and Gina. Jane and Sally barely noticed as Nancy slipped away.

Walking down the corridor, Nancy peered into room after room, looking unsuccessfully for Ned and Gina. Finally she checked her copy of the workshop schedule. The students were due to have lunch in fifteen minutes. She went back down the other corridor to the banquet room.

Slipping through the door, Nancy saw Bess laying silverware on the round tables. She spotted George, too, who looked up and waved Nancy in. With her short, dark, curly hair and athletic build, the lifeguard's warm-up outfit looked great on George.

"I'm on my lunch break," George said. "Any developments?" Nancy had filled her in about the case the night before, as the three girls settled into their hotel room.

Nancy shook her head. "The only thing developing around here is film in the students' darkroom," she quipped.

A tall, dark-haired young waiter appeared at George's side. "George, you know the rules—no socializing with the hotel guests," he said, wagging a finger teasingly at her. His hazel eyes sparkled.

"Cut it out, Paul," George said, grinning. "This is my friend, Nancy. Nancy, this is Paul Lampedusa."

As Nancy shook his hand, she noticed George blush. So, Nancy thought, George has already met a guy. Well, at least one of us is finding romance.

Just then Bess hurried over. "He's here again!" she moaned. George and Nancy looked toward a nearby doorway. Ralph, the bellman Nancy and Bess had met the previous afternoon, leaned into the room and waved at Bess.

"He won't leave me alone," Bess said through her teeth as she forced a smile. "I thought being at the hotel would help me see more of Gary Ruxton. I didn't bargain for a lovesick nerd!"

Soon the double doors swung open, and the students flooded in. Nancy, still on the lookout for Gina—and Ned—sat at a table by the door.

She'd just started to chat with the others at her table when she saw Sally Harvey in the doorway, camera case slung over her shoulder. Her face looked pale. Nancy jumped up and ran over to her. "Sally, what's wrong?" she asked.

Sally spoke in a small, tight voice. "Our room has been broken into—again!"

Leaving Sally where she was, Nancy found Bess, asked her to find Mr. Ruxton, then hurried off with Sally. "Gina returned to my class before lunch, and we went to drop off my cameras in the room," Sally explained in the elevator as the girls went up to the seventh floor. "When we got there, the door was open. Ned went in to check it out. Then he sent me down to get you."

Sally met Nancy's eyes. "Nancy—what if some kidnapper is after Gina? She's my best friend, you know. I'm so scared for her!"

"Then you're lucky Ned's around. He'll protect you," Nancy said reassuringly.

When they reached the room, Gina was sitting on the edge of her bed, looking visibly shaken. Ned sat on the bed beside her, one arm around her shoulders. When Nancy walked in, he threw her an apologetic glance. Seeing Gina's state, Nancy nodded her okay.

But, she thought to herself, Gina was awfully cool about last night's break-in. Why is she so upset this time? To get attention from Ned?

Examining the door, Nancy saw no sign of forced entry. But she thought that the room was much less a mess than it had been the night before. Had the thief found what he was looking for this time?

Then, on a hunch, Nancy went into the hall to

look for Rosita Ortiz. She found her in the nearest supply closet, sitting with her head in her hands. As Rosita raised her frightened face, Nancy saw she had been crying.

"What's the matter?" Nancy asked her.

"Oh, miss, it's you!" Rosita cried. "I didn't know where you were, but I had to tell you—I can't find my passkey!"

Chapter

Five

"Yᴏᴜʀ ᴘᴀssᴋᴇʏ ɪs ᴍɪssɪɴɢ?" Nancy asked Rosita, trying to sound calm. "When was the last time you had it?"

"Half an hour ago," Rosita said in a quivering voice. "A guest asked me to open his room. He said he left his card inside. In training they tell us never to use a passkey for a guest. We must say to go ask the front desk. But he was very nice."

Nancy drew a careful breath. "This man—what did he look like?"

Rosita looked scared. "He was not wearing a suit, just a shirt and pants," she said, struggling to remember. "Brown hair. American. Very tall."

Tall, Nancy thought. Like Nick Kessler? "Was it room 707?" she asked.

"Oh, no," Rosita declared. "After what happened yesterday, I would not open that door."

"You just let him in and left?" Nancy asked.

Rosita shook her head. "He needed me to help fix a closet door," she said. "It had come off the track. He and I both bent down to fix it. Maybe my key fell off then." She showed Nancy an empty key clip hooked to her belt. "I went back, but when I knocked, he was not there. So I looked here for my key." Rosita waved her hand, indicating the shelves of the supply closet. The sheets and towels were in disarray from her frantic search.

Nancy tried to imagine the scene in the man's room—two people bent down near the sliding doors of the closet, probably close together. It would have been easy for the man to slip the key off Rosita's key clip.

Nancy asked Rosita to show her which room the man had been in. She knew that it might not have been his real room—maybe he had asked Rosita to open any room, as a ruse to steal her passkey. But Nancy wanted to explore every possible lead.

Rosita and Nancy left the supply closet and wandered down the hall. Reaching the end, Rosita became flustered. "Maybe it was here," she said, stopping at room 724. Nancy knocked. No answer. "No, I think it was this one," Rosita continued, changing her mind. She went to room 726. "But . . . they all look the same," she said with a helpless shrug.

Disappointed, Nancy pulled a small notebook out of her purse. "Here's my name and room number," she said, writing them down and tear-ing out the page for Rosita. "If you see that man again, please call."

"I will," Rosita promised. "But please, miss, don't tell Mr. Wasilick I have lost my key!"

"I think you'd better report it," Nancy said. "You'll need a new key to get into the rooms to do your work. Mr. Wasilick can't blame you if the key was stolen from you. But I promise I won't tell anyone that you opened a room for a guest."

Rosita looked at Nancy gratefully. "Thank you!"

Nancy went back to her room and phoned Ms. Peabody for the names of the guests at the far end of the hall. None of the names were familiar, though she jotted them all down for future reference. Then she went downstairs and grabbed lunch at the mezzanine-level café. She knew Bess was still waiting tables, and George was back at the pool.

Next, after signing her room check, Nancy went to find Ned. She knew that Gina and Sally had workshops all afternoon. In a hallway outside the meeting rooms, Nancy finally spotted him, tipped back in a chair, reading a magazine. Seeing Nancy, he brought the chair down with a thump. "Hey, Drew, what's up?" he called to her happily.

Nancy mustered a smile, hoping she wouldn't look too uptight at seeing him. She sure *felt* uptight. "Hey, Ned. How's the bodyguard business?" she replied.

"Bor-*ring*," Ned complained.

"Look, Ned, I need to search Gina's room for clues," Nancy said. "Is that okay with you?"

"Sure," Ned replied. He pulled out two keycards from his pocket. "One's for my room, one is Gina's—I can't remember which is which. Take them both. Bring them back when you're done—I'll be here till four."

"Thanks," Nancy said, taking the cards. "See you then." With a little wave, she turned to walk away.

"Hey, Drew!" Ned called. Nancy turned. He tapped a finger on his lips. Slipping back, she bent over for a kiss. He reached up, caught her shoulders, and held her for a few extra seconds.

Nancy broke away. "I miss you," she murmured.

Ned nodded. "I miss you. Let's not let Gina catch us, huh?"

Nancy's face darkened. "Why not?" she asked.

Ned shrugged. "I thought we weren't supposed to let on we knew each other," he said casually.

"Oh, right," Nancy said. But as she left, she felt uneasy. Ned had seemed his old self again—until the remark about Gina. They both knew how Gina would have reacted if she'd seen them kissing.

Nancy went upstairs and started her search of Gina's room. She dusted for fingerprints on all doorknobs and drawer handles, but they were too smudged to read. She pulled a couple of snags of clothing fiber from a splintered edge of the desk. A quick check in the closet showed they were threads from Gina's clothes.

She sifted through the wastebaskets, looking for anything the thief might have discarded. But all she found was makeup-smeared cotton balls, an empty film container, and wrappers from the hotel chocolates left on guests' pillows each night.

Then, on a memo pad on the desk, Nancy spied dents in the paper, left by writing on the previous top sheet. Shading over it with pencil, she outlined the message:

Ned—Sweetest dreams. I feel so much safer knowing you're on the other side of my wall. If I get lonely during the night, can I call you?—G

Nancy tore off the paper and crumpled it up. So that's what is going on! she fumed.

Storming out of the room, Nancy went back downstairs. She knew Ned was waiting for his keycards, but she couldn't face him right now. Instead she found Bess in the Muskoka Lobby, setting up a snack table. Nancy asked her to return the keycards to Ned. "I have to check in with George," she added, not wanting to go into the real reason, and headed for the pool, which was on the roof of the hotel's three-story annex.

Wearing a red tank suit, George was walking along the pool with a screen on a long pole, skimming leaves from the water. "Nancy, put on your suit and go for a swim," George urged her. "You could use some relaxation. You look tense."

"And for good reason." Nancy groaned as she flopped down on a poolside chair. George sat beside her, and Nancy told her about the note she'd found in Gina's room.

George made a face. "You don't think Ned would fall for a gooey routine like that, do you?" she said. "Besides, you don't know that he's done anything to encourage her."

"She doesn't *need* encouraging," Nancy said, scowling. "And he obviously hasn't told her he's already involved. He's just eating up the attention."

"Of course he is. He's only human," George reminded her. "Look, Nan, I know this is hard for you. But you just have to trust the guy."

"I know, I know," Nancy said. "But seeing this little flirtation go on right under my nose is really frustrating."

"So what's going on with the case?" George asked. Nancy knew she was trying to get Nancy's mind off Ned, and it worked. By the time Nancy had recounted the day's developments, she felt calmer.

"Well, there's not much going on here," George said. "Not many people swim in the middle of the day." Scanning the pool, Nancy saw two ten-year-old boys playing tag in the shallow end, and one man swimming laps.

"Jane Sellery told me she always takes an

after-dinner swim," Nancy noted. "Watch for her this evening. She's tall, with red hair."

"I will," George commented.

The two girls fell silent, each wrapped up in her own thoughts. "I like the way they've planted those trees and shrubs around the sides of the terrace," Nancy finally said.

"That plant's a rhododendron—we have one like it in our backyard," George commented. "It's really pretty when the flowers bloom."

Nancy nodded, looking at the nearby bank of greenery. "And this one next to it is hemlock," she commented, fingering a small evergreen.

"Hemlock—like the poison?" George asked.

"No," Nancy said, "poison hemlock is an herb, with fine leaves. It looks almost like parsley. But speaking of poisons . . ." Nancy stood up to examine a narrow-leafed evergreen bush with white blossoms. "This is oleander. This *is* deadly."

"How do you detectives end up knowing so many grisly facts?" George declared with a shudder.

"I sat in once on a med school class on accidental poisoning," Nancy explained.

Just then out of the corner of her eye she saw the man who'd been swimming. He was sitting at a nearby table, drying his hair and beard with a towel. Nancy recognized him as the man who'd met Evan Sharpless on the mezzanine the day before.

Suddenly the man saw Nancy watching him.

Scooping up his clothes, he scurried into the men's locker room.

"That guy sure is acting strangely," Nancy said. "I saw him yesterday with Evan Sharpless."

"Maybe he's a reporter, too," George suggested. "Maybe he's leading a class. Why don't you ask him?"

"I will, if he comes back out," Nancy said.

"Why wait?" George asked. "Hang on, Nan, I'll try to find him." Before Nancy could protest, George marched boldly to the door of the men's locker room and called out for the attendant.

Impressed with George's resolve, Nancy sat waiting anxiously. She unconsciously snapped a twig from the oleander bush, watching the milky white sap ooze out. Then, remembering how poisonous the plant was, she tossed the twig into a litter basket.

Finally George returned. "Either he ran out the doorway leading to the hotel, or he's hiding somewhere inside," she said. "The attendant barely saw him run past."

Nancy laughed. "Well, thanks for trying. Anyway, what's next on your schedule?"

"I'm supposed to bus tables at a buffet dinner tonight," George said. "They need extra help. And I'm meeting Bess for dinner in the employee cafeteria. Why don't you come along and see how the other half lives?"

Agreeing, Nancy went with George back up to their room to change and relax for an hour or so. Then George led Nancy into the seventh-floor service corridor. "This is the route we workers have to take," George announced with a grin. Nancy recognized the area as the corridor Rosita had shown her. The two girls took the big, clunky service elevator down to the subbasement.

A hallway lined with metal lockers led from the elevator. Sidestepping a rolling hamper filled with dirty green coveralls, Nancy and George entered the cafeteria, a cement-floored room with harsh lighting. Paul Lampedusa waved to George from a table, and George waved back eagerly.

George and Nancy filled their plates and joined Paul. Bess soon arrived. As they all ate and chatted, Nancy decided Paul was funny, smart, and charming. She gathered that he was working here part-time to help pay his college tuition.

After dinner Paul gave the girls a tour of the hotel's immense kitchen, also in the subbasement. Gleaming white tile stretched for yards, along huge steel cooking ranges, counters, and banks of ovens. The walk-in refrigerators were as big as rooms. "The hotel has three restaurants and four banquet rooms," Paul explained. "On a good night, they could serve two thousand meals out of here."

Suddenly a man in a white coat leaned through a door. "Buffet ready—servers upstairs!" he barked.

Excusing themselves, Paul, George, and Bess jogged over to a small service elevator. Nancy noticed trolleys loaded with platters of food already on the elevator. The waiters stepped on and headed upstairs.

Nancy turned back again to marvel at the kitchen. A steel counter beside her was piled high with warming plates, ready to go up to the buffet. She noticed rice pilaf and a pile of shish kebabs —cubes of meat and vegetables cooked on long sticks.

Then Nancy saw a pile of slim peeled twigs beside a platter with more chunks of meat. Frowning, she picked one up and broke it open. A milky white sap came out.

Nancy rushed to find the nearest chef, a woman in a mushroom-shaped white hat. "Excuse me—where are those sticks from?" Nancy asked urgently.

"I don't know," the chef replied. "The shish kebabs are for the high-school kids. The menu theme *was* Wild West, but an hour ago the conference director sent us a note to make it Middle Eastern, too. He sent these wooden skewers down, saying they'd be more authentic."

"But you can't serve these shish kebabs," Nancy announced.

"Why not?" the chef asked, frowning.

"Those skewers are made from the oleander bush," Nancy said. "They're deadly poisonous!"

Chapter

Six

THE CHEF'S FACE froze in horror. "But we already sent up two platters of those shish kebabs," she said with a gasp. "They're upstairs now—being eaten!"

There wasn't a second to waste. Nancy raced to the service elevator and pounded the button with her fist. "Call upstairs and get someone to take those shish kebabs away!" she called back to the chef. "And then destroy the rest of those twigs—but not by burning them. Even the smoke is poisonous!"

Just then the elevator doors opened. Nancy strode in and pushed the button for the second floor, where she knew the banquet room was located. The elevator climbed upward at what seemed like a snail's pace. Nancy rapped on the wall in frustration.

Finally the doors opened onto a small pantry.

Nancy saw no shish kebabs on the counters. A phone on the wall was ringing—the chef must be trying to call upstairs, Nancy guessed. That meant that no one had yet been told about the deadly skewers. She sprang to the double doors leading to the banquet room and flung them open.

A throng of students milled around the room, everybody talking at once. Small round tables had been set up around the outer walls; a long buffet table took up the center of the room. A line of hungry students was moving up to the buffet table, and Nancy saw that about ten kids had already served themselves. Some held their plates and ate standing up. Others were sitting at the small tables.

Nancy shoved through the crowd to the buffet and spotted a tray of shish kebabs at the end of the table. She raced over.

Seizing the hot platter in her hands, Nancy yanked it off the table. She spotted George standing nearby holding a linen cloth, and she thrust the dish into George's hands. "Take these to the pantry and destroy them," Nancy said quickly. Without asking why, George instantly obeyed.

Grabbing a cloth napkin, Nancy ran to the other end of the buffet table, which had the same food laid out. She snatched the other shish kebab platter just as a student was reaching for a skewer. "Try the chicken wings instead," Nancy advised with a smile. She scurried to the pantry with the deadly dish.

"What's wrong with these?" George asked as Nancy came through the double doors.

"If we hadn't been talking about oleander this afternoon, I might not have noticed," Nancy said. She plunked the hot platter down on the counter. "But these skewers are oleander twigs. The poison would seep through the bark and taint the food. I just hope no one's eaten any yet!"

Hurrying back to the banquet room, Nancy hunted frantically for Gary Ruxton. She spied him near the buffet line, chatting with Evan Sharpless. As she rushed up, the teacher smiled at her. "Nancy Drew!" he said. "I was just telling Mr. Sharpless about our mystery—"

"Mr. Ruxton," Nancy interrupted, a bit annoyed that he was blowing her cover, "could you make an emergency announcement?"

"Of course," Mr. Ruxton said. As he and Nancy threaded their way through the crowd to a podium, she explained the situation.

A moment later Mr. Ruxton spoke into the microphone. "Attention, students," he began. The room fell silent. "Anyone who took a shish kebab from the buffet, please do not eat it." A ripple of excitement ran through the crowd. "Anyone who has already eaten some should come see me immedia—"

At that very moment, a boy across the room doubled over. Nancy saw Jane Sellery standing beside him. As the boy began to collapse, Jane screamed.

Nancy rushed to the boy's side, but Evan Sharpless was already there. Supporting the boy by the arm, the reporter twisted around, clearly looking for help. Nancy saw Bess standing behind him, her mouth gaping open.

"Waitress, get a doctor!" Mr. Sharpless ordered Bess. "There's a cardiologist staying here —he spoke to me in the lobby earlier. He's in room 555, I remember. Call him." Nodding, Bess ran off to a phone.

Nancy leaned over to speak to Mr. Sharpless. "The poison was oleander," she told him. "It has effects similar to digitalis poisoning."

The newscaster turned to take in Nancy with a shrewd, appraising glance. "Thanks—that'll help," he said. "When I was in the service in Vietnam, I saw a few cases of accidental poisoning. I know these first few minutes are critical."

The sick boy raised his head weakly, gasping for air. Mr. Sharpless helped him to his feet. Half carrying the boy, the reporter moved him out of the banquet room. As Nancy followed, she spotted Gina near the door, surrounded by several guys from the workshop. Sally stood awkwardly behind her, anxiously twisting her brown curls.

Ned, leaning against the wall outside the banquet room door, looked up as Mr. Sharpless helped the sick boy to a sofa in a nearby lounge area.

Soon the doctor arrived, out of breath from having hurried to the scene. He frowned as he felt the boy's pulse.

"Most likely a case of oleander poisoning," Mr. Sharpless told him. "Apparently, it's like digitalis poisoning."

The doctor nodded. Reaching into his medical case, he pulled out a vial of medicine and started to fill a hypodermic needle. "His heart's beating a mile a minute," he said. "Quinidine should help."

A few moments later, a crew of paramedics arrived, in response to Bess's call. Nancy stepped away to let them through.

Nancy decided the situation was under control and made her way back to the banquet room. Passing Ned again, Nancy paused and filled him in on what had happened to the boy. Ned asked when Nancy had finished, "Gina's okay?"

Nancy fought down a jealous reflex. "Of course—why wouldn't she be?" she snapped.

Ned looked surprised. "Well, I just assumed that whoever did this was trying to get at her. After all the other stuff—"

"That *is* possible," Nancy admitted. "But I don't want to leap to conclusions. I'll let you know what I find out." And she hurried back into the banquet room.

The room was still buzzing with excited conversation. Gary Ruxton, hovering anxiously near the door, stopped her. "How is he?" he asked.

"He looks better," Nancy said guardedly.

"What an awful accident," Mr. Ruxton moaned.

"Or—maybe it wasn't an accident," Nancy

said. Looking over her shoulder to make sure no one was listening, she leaned toward Mr. Ruxton. "The chef told me you ordered those shish kebabs."

Ruxton looked disturbed. "I did call the banquet director, and I asked to add some Middle Eastern food for tonight," he admitted. "At lunch Evan Sharpless was telling some students about covering the Middle East. On the spur of the moment, he offered to speak about the Middle East to the whole workshop tonight—at no charge. His speaking fees are enormous, so it seemed like a real treat."

"He seems very involved with the students," Nancy noted. "I'm impressed that he's so interested."

"He's a great guy," the teacher agreed. "Anyway, he suggested that the dinner food could tie in to the speech. I don't recall anyone mentioning shish kebabs. There were lots of people around, though."

"Including Jane Sellery?" Nancy asked.

Mr. Ruxton, looking surprised, nodded. "How do you know Jane Sellery?" he asked.

"I talked to her last night. She and Gina Fiorella know each other," Nancy said, trying to sound concommittal. "But if no one mentioned shish kebabs, why did you send the oleander skewers to the chef?"

Mr. Ruxton's face was blank. "I didn't," he said.

Nancy straightened up. "The chef said she got a note from you, with the skewers," she said.

"Why would I do that?" he asked, puzzled.

Nancy's mind raced. "I'd better go check out a few details," she said. "I'll report back later." She turned and walked swiftly back to the service elevator, which took her down to the kitchen again.

Questioning the chef, Nancy got the whole story. The bundle of skewers had simply appeared on the counter, the woman said, with a note attached. The chef showed it to Nancy. Typed on hotel stationery, it had Gary Ruxton's name typed at the bottom, but no handwritten signature.

Keeping the note for evidence, Nancy went next to the swimming pool level. Whoever put those skewers in the kitchen didn't have to go far for them, she reasoned. Any hotel guest could have found them—right by the pool. She thought at once of the man with the beard who'd run away from her at the pool earlier.

Emerging onto the pool terrace, she crossed over to the oleander bushes. Though the sun was going down, floodlights lit up the terrace, and Nancy knelt to inspect the shrubs. Soon she found a patch of oleander with several branches hacked away. Milky sap still oozed from the cuts. The cutting was recent.

Nancy walked back to the elevators, deep in thought. Why would anyone do something so dangerous—risking the lives of many young people? And *was* this crime related to Gina Fiorella's incidents?

She considered her two main suspects so far. It was hard to believe that Jane Sellery would go this far just to settle a school rivalry. Nick Kessler might be angry about Gina firing him, but would he have hurt Gina? He did seem to have a crush on her, though; would he have hurt other people for Gina's sake?

Nancy decided to return to her room so she could think about the case without being disturbed. Taking the elevator up to her floor, she strolled down the hall, thinking about where all the clues left her. It was still possible that Gina's father's enemies were behind everything. From what she'd heard, they might be the kind of people who would hurt a banquet full of students. Was the bearded guy working for them?

Unlocking her door, Nancy stepped inside. The red message light was flashing on her phone. She crossed to the phone, lifted the receiver, and punched the button to retrieve the call. Then she listened for the recorded message her caller had left.

It was a deep voice, probably a man's, Nancy figured. It sounded harsh and gravelly—and very frightening.

The voice snarled, "Keep your nose out of things that don't concern you, Nancy Drew!"

Chapter

Seven

NANCY FROZE, the phone receiver in her hand, as the message lapsed into a dial tone. The anonymous caller's threat still rasped in her ear. Whoever was behind all this knew who she was now. And clearly this was someone who would stop at nothing to achieve his or her goal.

But what was that goal?

Nancy called the hotel's operator. "This is Nancy Drew, in room 714," she said. "I just picked up a phone message I didn't understand. Could you tell me who left it?"

"I'm sorry," the operator said. "Our system is fully automated. No operator talks to the caller, and there's no record of the call."

"Thanks anyway," Nancy said, and hung up. "The marvels of modern technology—it only makes things easier for criminals," she muttered to herself.

Nancy glanced around the room to make sure her caller hadn't left any other surprises for her. Then she checked her watch. It was almost eight o'clock. The dinner was probably ending now, but Bess and George would be cleaning up for at least an hour. She didn't feel like staying here alone—not after that call. She decided to go find Ned.

Stepping back into the hallway, Nancy headed for the elevators. As she turned the corner, she saw Jane Sellery. Nancy's mind flashed to an image of Jane at the banquet, standing by the stricken boy, mouth open in horror. Jane's behavior suggested that she was shocked by the poisoning, but Nancy knew that Jane could be playacting. Nancy noticed that Jane was still wearing the dress she had worn at dinner, but now she had a towel over her shoulder.

"Hi," Nancy said brightly. "Going for your swim?"

Jane looked startled to see Nancy. "Uh—yes," she answered.

Nancy raised an eyebrow. "But the pool is on the third level," she pointed out. "And your room is on six, isn't it?"

Jane's eyes widened. "I was just . . . just . . . looking for a friend whose room is up here," she stammered. "Well, maybe she'll come on down to the pool and meet me there. 'Bye." Jane scooted into the elevator that had just arrived.

Nancy, curious, watched her go. The arrow-shaped light above the elevator showed it was going up, not down to the pool level. Was Jane really going to the pool and had just gotten into an up elevator by mistake? Why had she made up that lame story about looking for a friend? Jane definitely was behaving strangely.

Remembering that George wasn't scheduled to lifeguard that night, Nancy decided to drop by the pool to check Jane's alibi. She pressed the Down button, and an elevator arrived instantly.

A big, burly man in jeans and a sweatshirt was getting off. It was Nick Kessler! Why was he still hanging around the hotel?

Seeing Nancy, the bodyguard looked alarmed. He hopped back into the elevator and jabbed a button. Nancy was so surprised that she didn't move. The elevators doors slid shut, leaving her behind.

Nancy frowned. Clearly Nick Kessler knew who she was. Could *he* have left that message on her phone?

Was Nick Kessler the one harassing Gina? He certainly knew the ins and outs of the hotel, Nancy mused. And he had a motive: he'd been pretty upset at losing his job guarding Gina.

Then another thought struck Nancy. Could Nick Kessler have been paid off by Mr. Fiorella's enemies to hurt Gina? Was he working with the bearded man?

A shiver ran through Nancy. Luckily, no one has been seriously hurt—yet, she thought. But she had an ominous feeling that something bad would happen—and soon.

Just then another Down elevator arrived and Nancy stepped in. She pressed the button for the third floor and proceeded to the pool. Glancing through a picture window in the corridor, she saw Jane Sellery emerge from the locker room, tugging a swim cap down over her red hair. Well, at least that story is true, Nancy thought.

But Nancy's mind was still on Nick Kessler. She decided to go to the lobby. She went downstairs and asked the front desk clerk whether a Nick Kessler was staying there. He checked the register and said no.

Nancy drifted over to one of the side alcoves and dropped into a leather armchair. Here, she knew, she could see without being seen. If the bodyguard didn't have a room in the hotel, he'd have to walk through the lobby at some point, Nancy figured, and she'd keep her eyes peeled for the man in the beard, too. Maybe he was just a friend of Evan Sharpless, but then why had he run away from her that afternoon?

An hour came and went. The lobby was a constant parade of people—meeting, mingling, going out for the evening, coming in for the night. Flocks of students from the workshop went by, chatting eagerly. But Nancy saw no sign of Nick Kessler or the bearded man.

Finally, Gary Ruxton came strolling across the lobby. The boy who'd been sick at the banquet was with him, along with an anxious-looking blond woman—the boy's mother, Nancy guessed. The boy looked fine now, but Nancy knew it had been a close call. She felt sorry for Mr. Ruxton. This workshop had been nothing but headaches for him so far.

Then she saw Bess, in her waitress uniform, walking a few paces behind Mr. Ruxton. The wistful, adoring expression on her face was too much. Nancy stood up and darted behind a lush potted fern, spying on her friend.

As Bess passed near the footbridge over the pool, Ralph trotted down the steps from the front door and grabbed Bess's hand. Bess twisted around and stared at him in panic. She yanked her hand away, but Ralph went on jabbering ardently. Meanwhile, Mr. Ruxton had turned to go up the steps and out the front door. Seeing him leave, Bess collapsed with a sigh.

Nancy smothered a smile. Then she saw that Ralph had actually convinced Bess to go somewhere with him, because the two disappeared down a side hallway. Nancy stretched her limbs and straightened up. She wasn't having any luck finding her suspects, so she decided she might as well go back to her room. If Bess was off duty, maybe George was, too. She decided to check upstairs.

Stepping off the elevator on the seventh floor, she looked down toward room 707. Ned was stationed on a folding chair outside Gina's door, drinking from a can of soda. Realizing she never did get to find him earlier, Nancy decided to go tell him what she'd learned about the oleander skewers.

As she headed down the hall, Nancy felt her pulse speed up. Ned looked up, saw her, waved, and grinned. Nancy broke into a grin, too. I'm not being fair to Ned, she told herself. Her stride quickened.

But just then, the door to Room 707 opened. Gina leaned out, hanging seductively on the doorjamb. Her glossy dark hair swung alluringly over her face.

Nancy felt her entire body go rigid. She half hid in a doorway, a few yards away.

"Ned," Gina cooed, "I'm *hungry*. I just couldn't eat a bite at dinner, not after what happened to that poor boy. I thought I'd order a plate of pasta from room service. Can I get you anything? I feel so bad for you, stuck out here."

Ned smiled up at Gina. Watching him, Nancy thought how much she loved the way his eyes crinkled at the corners when he smiled—and how awful it was to see those eyes crinkling at someone else.

"Thanks, Gina, I'm fine," Ned told her. "Sally brought me a huge plate of food from the buffet —no shish kebabs, luckily," he added with a chuckle.

Gina pouted. "Can't I get you something to drink from the minibar?" she asked.

Ned shook his head. "I just got a soda from the vending machine." He showed her the can. "Thanks, anyway."

Shrugging her delicate shoulders, Gina swung back into the room and slammed the door. Ned looked guiltily at Nancy. "She's a very thoughtful employer," he said, joking weakly.

Nancy tried to look unconcerned as she walked up to him. "Maybe I should check out that room-service order before she gets it," she suggested. "If our culprit is willing to poison a whole banquet—"

"I'll check the food when it gets here," Ned said. "Go look around the hotel. I've got things covered here."

Nancy drew back, hurt. "This is a very clever person we're dealing with," she argued. "And he—or she—clearly knows how to operate in the kitchen downstairs. It wouldn't be hard to find out about that room-service order and poison it."

"Yes, Nancy, but this is my job," Ned said. "Or don't you think I'm up to it?"

A hurt silence fell between them. Their eyes met. "It's not that—" Nancy began weakly.

Ned's voice lowered. "Or don't you trust me being around Gina? That's really it, Nan, isn't it?"

Nancy felt her ears burn. Ned knew her so well! She hated to admit that she could be thrown off balance by jealousy, but she was.

Nancy sighed. "It's Gina I don't trust," she said. "But that doesn't mean I won't do my best to solve this mystery." She spun around and walked away. She didn't dare look back at Ned.

Turning down the service corridor, Nancy pushed the button to call the service elevator. It took her down to the kitchen. Even though it was past dinnertime, the kitchen was still a hive of activity.

Paul Lampedusa, working at a nearby counter, waved. "Hi, Nancy, what's cooking?" he joked.

Nancy strolled over to join him. "Still working?"

"I'm on the night owl room-service shift," Paul explained. "It's a choice assignment—you get good tips. Banquet waiters get no tips at all."

"That's a coincidence—a friend of mine just called down an order for room service," Nancy said, trying to keep her cover. "Room 707?"

Paul leaned over and looked at several slips of paper clipped to a chrome strip on the wall. "Yeah, here it is," he said. "Angel hair pasta with pesto sauce. Only she wants us to substitute linguine for the angel hair, hold the pesto sauce, toss it with olive oil, and send up parmesan cheese on the side. *Freshly grated* parmesan." He rolled his eyes. "She's a friend of yours? Stick with friends like George and you'll be better off."

Nancy laughed. "Well, Gina's not really a friend," she said vaguely. Just then a chef pushed a plate of linguine over the counter from a side kitchen area. "That must be her order now," Nancy added. "Mind if I check it out? I mean, if she's going to be picky . . ."

Paul laughed. "Be my guest."

Nancy took a fork and lifted a strand of the pasta. She sniffed it, then dabbed the end on her tongue. Everything seemed okay. Next she spooned through the small bowl of parmesan cheese Paul had set on a tray beside the pasta. The cheese also checked out fine.

Paul covered the pasta with a dome-shaped silver lid and hefted the tray onto his shoulder. "Looks like you're trying out for the Secret Service. Want to come up with me?" he asked.

Nancy nodded and started toward the elevator. At that moment Stan Wasilick bustled up. "Ms. Drew, it's bad enough you meddle with my work," he complained. "But when you help employees break the rules—"

Nancy turned to Paul. "You go on up," she said quickly, hoping her cover wasn't completely blown. Paul shrugged and went into the service elevator. Nancy turned back to the security chief.

"I interrogated Rosita Ortiz in my office for twenty minutes about how she lost her passkey," he said. "She finally cracked and told me she had let a guest without a keycard into his room. *And* she said that *you* had told her it wasn't her fault."

Nancy sighed. "I was just trying to calm her down after her passkey was stolen," she said. "And no one can prove that the intruder used her passkey to get into room 707. Now, if you'll excuse me—" She slipped away and hurried down the wide center aisle of the kitchen. Using her good sense of direction, she found her way to the passenger elevator and rode to the seventh floor.

Striding down the hallway, Nancy uneasily noted that Ned wasn't outside Gina's room. Just then she saw Paul enter the hall from the service corridor and turn toward room 707. Reaching the door, he balanced his tray on one shoulder and knocked.

The door opened and Ned leaned out. Hmmm, Nancy thought. Why was Ned in Gina's room?

Then Gina poked her head around Ned's shoulder. "Oh, good, my pasta!" she exclaimed. Her hand reached out to pull the silver cover off the plate.

As she lifted the lid, Nancy saw Gina's expression change. With a look of horror on her face, she dropped the lid and screamed, knocking the tray out of Paul's hands. Nancy ran forward.

Pushing past Paul, Nancy saw the mess on the floor. A mass of slippery linguine lay plopped on the corridor carpet—with a dead rat on top!

Chapter

Eight

GINA WAS SHRIEKING and hopping up and down. Her hands clawed wildly at Ned's shoulder. He put both of his hands on her upper arms and held her tightly. "Calm down, calm down," he kept saying.

Behind them Sally Harvey came to the door and peeked out. Paul was already on his hands and knees, trying to clear up the pasta. Sally, seeing the rat, scrunched up her face. "Yuck!" she said softly.

"Look," Nancy said to Sally, seeing that she was calmer than Gina. "The rat could be a ploy to get you out of the room for some reason. You two may want to go somewhere else, but I think Ned should stand guard while you're away."

Still holding Gina, Ned said, "There's no way I'll leave her alone. What if these guys are armed, Nancy? I can't leave her unprotected."

"But, Ned," Nancy argued, "if they're armed, why didn't they shoot her yesterday, instead of just knocking her into the pool?"

Gina jerked around to look at Ned, then Nancy. "Hey, do you two know each other?" she asked suspiciously.

"River Heights is a small town—everybody knows everybody here," Ned answered quickly. "Look, do you still want pasta? Let's go down to the café. You'll feel better once you've eaten something."

Gina, still looking wild-eyed, nodded numbly. "We'll just freshen up a bit," Sally said, and shut the door.

Nancy chewed her lip, feeling frustrated. "You really shouldn't leave the room unprotected," she told Ned.

"I'm in charge here!" Ned snapped. "And I'll decide. I'll have hotel security send someone to watch outside while we're gone. In fact, I'll go call right now." He wheeled around and stomped over to his room. From the way he jammed the keycard into the door, Nancy could tell he was furious with her.

Good work, Drew, she thought miserably. By trying to keep Ned away from Gina, you've made him so mad he'll go straight into her arms.

Paul, kneeling on the carpet as he cleaned up the mess, looked up at Nancy. "I know I'm just the waiter," he said lightly, "but would you mind telling me what's going on?"

With an effort, Nancy concentrated once more

on the case. She considered Paul's question. She liked Paul, but she didn't want to blow her cover. "My friend had her room broken into last night and again today," she said. "So her bodyguard's a little jumpy. I do wonder where this rat came from, though," she said with a hint of suspicion in her voice. "You and I both saw the plate in the kitchen, and there was nothing there then."

"Beats me," Paul declared. "Maybe someone tampered with it in the service elevator."

"Who was on the elevator with you?" Nancy asked.

Paul sat back on his heels, as he tried to remember. "One of the maintenance staff," he said. "You know, those guys in the green outfits. I don't know his name. The hotel's only been open a week, so we don't all know one another yet."

"Where did he get on?" Nancy asked.

"In the subbasement, where I got on," Paul said. "I was just about to go up, and he came running, wheeling one of those big laundry carts."

"Did he speak to you?" she asked.

"He asked me to push a button for him—ten, I think," Paul said. "And then—" He paused.

"Go on," Nancy said, encouraging him.

"He was fiddling with the cart, trying to get it straight," Paul said. "He said a wheel was caught in a floor crack, and he asked me to help. I set down my tray to do it. Then he accidentally jammed me into a corner for a minute. He may have had time to slip the rat under the cover then."

Nancy crossed her arms. "What did this guy look like?" she asked intently.

Paul shrugged. "Medium height and build, brown hair," he recalled slowly. "No, taller than medium height—those coveralls make everyone look shorter."

"Did he have a beard?" Nancy asked.

Paul ran a hand through his short dark hair. "To tell you the truth, Nancy, I hardly noticed him. He was just a guy in the elevator, you know?"

Nancy sighed. Paul's account tallied somewhat with Rosita's description of the man who probably stole her passkey. But both descriptions were too vague to be useful. The profile matched Nick Kessler, and possibly the bearded man, but it also matched half the men in River Heights, including her own father!

Just then Nancy noticed Ralph Winkler sauntering down the hallway with a goofy grin on his face. He waved at them. "Mr. Wasilick said I should come to 707," he announced. "Someone needs a guard?"

Ned's door opened, and he stepped out, pointedly avoiding Nancy's gaze. "Yeah, I called for a guard," he answered. Looking at Ralph's skinny body in his crimson bellman's uniform, Ned paused. "You sure you can handle this?" he asked.

Ralph rolled his eyes. "What's to handle?" he asked. "I can sit on a chair and stare at a door as well as anybody."

Ned looked annoyed at the job description. Nancy hid her smile.

Gina's door opened, and the two girls came out, looking a bit less upset. Ned escorted them down the hallway, without a word to Nancy. Saying goodbye to Paul, Nancy headed for her room.

As she came through the door, she saw Bess lying on the bed, watching TV. "Where've you been?" she asked.

Nancy ran through the details of the latest incident. Bess shivered when Nancy described the dead rat on the pasta. "How revolting!" she squealed.

Nancy finished her story. "Nick Kessler is the only suspect we have right now," she added. "And possibly a medium-height guy with a brown beard. You and George will have to keep your eyes open. Where is George, anyway?"

"At the pool," Bess said.

Nancy frowned. "She wasn't on duty tonight," she said.

"I know, but she went anyway," Bess explained. "She knew you wanted her to check out Jane Sellery."

"Good for George," Nancy declared. "Want to go down and join her for a swim?"

Bess shook her head stubbornly. "No way—

not if Ralph is down the hall," she said. "He's been following me all day. He's unshakable!"

Nancy giggled. "Maybe I should hire Ralph to tail suspects for me," she joked.

"It's not funny, Nancy," Bess said. "I'm dying to go down to the lobby for a candy bar, but I don't want to see him. And you know, if I give up chocolate for anything, it's really a big deal." Her expression shifted. "But now that you're here, Nan—will you go down and buy it for me?"

"No chance, Bess!" Nancy exclaimed. "I won't buy a candy bar for you. I'll go down with you, if you want, but I'm not feeding your cravings."

Bess moaned and hauled herself off the bed. "Okay, then, let's go," she said. "I guess if Ralph has to stay on that chair, he can't bother me."

Opening the door furtively, Nancy and Bess slipped out into the hall. Immediately, they heard Ralph hiss to get Bess's attention. "Sorry, Ralph, I'm in a hurry," Bess called, sprinting by him. The girls scuttled to the safety of the elevator bank.

Once downstairs, Nancy and Bess entered the gift shop, which was just off the lobby. Nancy flipped aimlessly through a magazine. "Hey, Nan, look at this," Bess called from behind a display rack. Nancy looked over.

Bess was holding up a huge T-shirt in an ugly greenish-tan color. Kiss Me, I'm Available, the caption read. Underneath was a drawing of a hideous pink octopus with eight circling arms.

"We should buy this for our pal Gina," Bess said, giggling.

"Come on, Bess, that's awful," Nancy said, but she smiled. It sure helped to know that her friends were on her side.

Bess bought two candy bars—"In case I get hungry later," she explained—and the two girls went back to the elevator bank. Nancy pushed the button and then glanced up at the mezzanine café. There, at a table right by the railing, Ned was sitting with Gina and Sally. All three were laughing and talking. Nancy seethed. "If he's so worried about assassins, why did he choose a table out in the open like that?" she said.

Just then a piercing whistle rang through the atrium. Nancy and Bess craned their necks to look up. Leaning over the seventh-floor railing, Ralph was madly waving his arm. He blew a kiss to Bess, then gestured urgently for her to come upstairs.

"I could die, I could just *die,*" whined Bess, scrunching up her body to seem as small as possible.

"Why don't I go and see what he wants?" Nancy said as an elevator came. "It may have to do with the case, anyway."

Bess nodded. "I'm just going to stay here and stuff myself with chocolate," she announced with a groan.

Nancy stepped into the elevator. When she reached seven, she called down the hall to Ralph as she approached him. "Everything okay?"

"Oh, sure," Ralph said, toying with the braid on his uniform shoulder. "But I just thought I should tell someone. A maintenance worker came to the room to fix the light in the bathroom. I didn't know anything about it, so I sent him away. Did I do right? I don't want Mr. Wasilick to get mad at me."

"You did just right," Nancy assured him. "What did the guy look like?"

Ralph looked confused. "Uh—brown hair. Not too tall," he said.

Was it the same man Rosita and Paul had run into? Nancy wondered. Nick Kessler? The bearded man? "Let me just look around to check things out," she said.

"By the way, did he have a beard?"

"Uh . . . I can't remember," Ralph answered, struggling to remember. "Well, I'll see you in a bit." Leaving Ralph, she went around the corner and walked through the open steel doors to the service corridor. Near the elevator she spied green coveralls tossed carelessly on the floor.

She knelt quickly beside them. Nancy bet that whoever had discarded them wasn't one of the hotel's real workers. She held them up, looking for clues.

Suddenly the corridor light went off. A second later, the steel doors slammed shut with a heavy clatter. Nancy was plunged into darkness, without a single ray of light to see by.

Then, outside, a high-pitched siren went off.

A fire alarm! Nancy was trapped.

Chapter

Nine

ON THE OTHER SIDE of the steel doors, Nancy heard people shouting and footsteps pounding as the fire alarm wailed on. She also heard several loud metallic clangs—probably more fire doors swinging shut, Nancy guessed. The noises echoed and reechoed throughout the hotel.

From arson cases she had worked on, Nancy knew that a series of fire doors should clap shut as soon as an alarm went off. Held shut by heavy springs, the doors would contain any fire in each sealed-off area. She had no hope of opening these doors by herself.

She groped along the wall to the service elevator and pushed the button. Pressing her ear to the door, she listened for cables and gears turning in the shaft. She heard nothing. Then she quickly remembered that once a fire alarm sounds, all elevators are halted. Otherwise, the shafts could become vertical fire tunnels, channeling flames and smoke to other floors.

Discouraged, Nancy realized that someone had hoped she would come in here to investigate Ralph's report about a maintenance worker. Slumping onto the floor, she sat in the dark. Had that same person switched off the light and pulled the fire alarm, knowing she would be trapped completely?

Then another possibility occurred to her. What if the alarm wasn't a fake? What if there really was a fire? Could this enclosed compartment become a death trap? The hotel's fire system had most likely not yet been tested in a real fire, she thought in horror.

Nancy fought down a wave of fear. Yes, she was trapped, but she didn't have to sit in the dark, she reasoned. If she could find the wall switch, she could turn the lights back on. She rose and began to feel her way along the wall.

Just then the fire siren stopped. With a crackle of static, a voice came over the loudspeaker system. It was Maureen Peabody's.

"Attention, guests," Ms. Peabody said. "Please do not panic. A fire alarm has been pulled on the seventh floor. No smoke detectors have gone off, and no actual fire has been spotted. However, in the interest of safety, all people are to walk down the fire stairs to the lobby. Do *not* use the elevators. Take the stairs. Repeat: No fire has been spotted."

The smoke detectors didn't go off, Nancy realized—a good sign that this was a false alarm.

Her fingers brushed against a light switch on the wall. She snapped the switch, and the corridor lit up. Looking around, she saw nothing unusual.

Then she heard heavy footsteps running outside, heading up the corridor. Deep male voices shouted orders. "Go to the far end and work your way back. Open every door." "Break 'em down?" "No, we have a key from the manager—here." It must be a crew of firefighters, Nancy thought. Pounding her fists against the fire door, she tried to catch their attention.

"Hey, someone's in here!" a voice shouted nearby. The firefighter came closer and called to Nancy. "You okay in there?"

"Yes," Nancy called back. "Can you get me out?"

"We can't disable the fire doors until we're sure there's no fire," the firefighter explained. "We're doing a room-to-room search. It'll take about five more minutes. Then we'll turn off the system. You'll be safe. Can you wait till then?"

"Sure," Nancy said uneasily. She knew she had no choice.

Leaning against the door, she willed herself to stay calm. They're just playing it safe, she thought. There's no fire.

But then, out in the corridor, she heard a firefighter shout. "We've found a blaze! Room 707!"

Nancy's heart leapt. Gina's room!

More footsteps pounded past. Nancy paced restlessly around her enclosed space. Her own fear had given way to worry about Gina. Whether or not she liked her, Nancy had to admit the girl was in danger.

Finally, Nancy heard the firefighters troop back out. The fire doors suddenly swung open, and Nancy sprinted into the corridor.

Looking down over the railing, she saw the lobby packed with anxious guests and staff members. A group of firefighters, in black coats and thick rubber boots, were gathering at the front entrance. A fire captain was conferring with Maureen Peabody. Evan Sharpless stood behind her.

Nancy saw the manager nod as he shook the captain's hand. Then she spoke to Mr. Sharpless. He turned and jogged to the bridge arching over the lobby pool.

When Evan Sharpless held up his hand for attention, the crowd fell silent. He called out in his resonant voice, "A small blaze was found and put out. All rooms have been checked and given the all clear. You may go back to your rooms now."

A spontaneous cheer arose from the crowd. Somehow, the newscaster's manner had put them at ease. Nancy guessed that was why Maureen Peabody had let him make the announcement.

Nancy ran down the hall to Gina's room. The

door stood wide open, and she saw at once the smoke-blackened door frame around the closet and the mass of charred clothing inside. The room smelled of smoke, but nothing else seemed to have burned.

At that moment Gina, Sally, and Ned came up behind Nancy. Gina gasped. "All our clothes are ruined!" she cried.

"You must have been downstairs when the fire started," Nancy said.

Sally turned to give Nancy an odd look. "No," she said. "We'd just come back upstairs when the alarm went off. We evacuated our room, but . . . there was no fire here when we left."

Nancy's eyes narrowed. "Then it *was* a false alarm," she said. "A way to get you out of your room and make sure no one would stay to guard the room. Someone must have sneaked in and set the fire after you left."

"Looks to me like someone wants to harass Gina but not necessarily hurt her," Ned said. "Burning up her clothes is one definite way to disturb her."

"Sally, maybe you and Gina should check to see that nothing else is ruined," Nancy suggested. Nodding, Sally moved slowly into the room.

"My best things!" Gina wailed, standing in front of the closet. "My shoes, my handbags. I'd just spent two days at the best boutiques in Rome. My whole wardrobe is gone!"

"Has anybody seen my camera?" Sally piped up uneasily. "I had a black canvas bag with a camera, all my lenses, several rolls of film, and a matching portfolio, too, full of developed negatives. It's all my photography stuff."

Ned, Nancy, and Gina began to hunt with Sally. "You had it with you at the café, I know," Gina said, peering behind the curtains. "She never goes anywhere without her camera," she added, looking at Nancy and Ned. Then Gina turned toward Sally. "I saw you bring it back up, Sal."

"I left it on the floor by the desk," Sally said. "It's definitely gone!"

Gina ran over to hug Sally. "Oh, I feel so horrible!" she said. "I can always buy more clothes, but your pictures can never be replaced." For once, Gina seemed more concerned with someone else's problem than with her own, Nancy realized.

"Maybe they'll turn up," Nancy said, trying to console Sally. "Right now, why don't I go get some clothes to lend you two? That way, you'll have something to wear tomorrow, at least."

"Gee, thanks, Nancy," Sally said gratefully.

"That'd be great," Gina chimed in. "And I'll take you shopping tomorrow, Sally. I'll buy you a new camera, and lots of new clothes."

"You don't need to, Gina," Sally protested.

"But it's all my fault!" Gina said. "Besides, I've always wanted to help you spruce up your wardrobe. I've got my credit cards. Daddy will never notice if I run up a little bill."

As Gina chattered on, Nancy saw that she was

successfully cheering up Sally. Gina may be a flirt, Nancy thought, but at least she's a loyal friend. And that was one trait Nancy admired in people.

Nancy quietly left and went down the hall to her room to fetch some clothes. Bess and George were both there and listened intently to Nancy's news of the fire. "Oh, let me help find clothes for Gina," Bess said with a sly grin.

Fifteen minutes later Nancy returned to room 707 with an armload of clothing. Ned was sitting on his chair outside room 709, next door. "I let them move into my room," he told Nancy. "I don't mind sleeping next to a burned closet, but Gina shouldn't have to. You were right, by the way. It *was* more important to guard the room than to guard Gina. I should have listened to you."

Nancy softened. "How could we guess what this maniac is up to?" she said. "I still don't understand him. Anyway, here are the clothes."

Ned rose and took the pile. Tossing it on his chair, he began to sort through it. There were a couple of George's sweatsuits, Bess's baggiest cotton shorts, and some T-shirts from the gift shop. Ned unfolded the one with the octopus on it. " 'Kiss Me, I'm Available,' " he read out loud. "Let me guess." He turned to Nancy with a grin. "Is this one for Gina, by any chance?"

Nancy feigned innocence. "Think it'll fit her?"

Ned laughed and drew Nancy into his arms. As

they melted into a long kiss, Nancy forgot to wonder whether anyone was watching.

Nancy and Bess were eating breakfast in the employee cafeteria the next morning, when George walked up, looking glum. "Bad news," she said. "Paul was fired."

Bess set down her tea cup with a clatter. "Why?" she asked with concern.

"Apparently he left work without permission last night," George said, sighing. "I just saw him down in the employees' locker area, clearing out his stuff. I'm going to meet him outside in ten minutes. Could you guys come, too? Maybe we can help him get his job back."

Nancy and Bess agreed. Clearing away their trays, the three girls went up a back staircase and emerged at the parking lot behind the hotel.

Paul was loading a duffel bag into the trunk of a small black car. At Nancy's urging, he told them his story.

"Mr. Wasilick was looking for me last night, around ten o'clock," he said. "I guess he wanted to grill me about the dead rat, since I was the one who delivered it. But I wasn't around, and he got steamed. And then the fire alarm went off."

"That was just after ten," Nancy commented.

Paul shrugged. "I came back at eleven-fifteen, after the fire was over. Wasilick had already gone home. When I came in this morning, he was waiting for me—to fire me for dereliction of duty. I got the idea he thought *I* pulled the alarm and set the fire."

Nancy looked at Paul steadily. "Did you?"

Paul seemed offended. "Of course not!" he declared. "Look, I shouldn't have left work, but I had a personal matter to attend to. I've got an alibi."

"Where were you?" Nancy asked, pressing him.

"An old girlfriend called and asked to meet me for a cup of coffee over on campus," he began. "She said it was urgent. She told me her little sister is at the yearbook conference, and she'd heard there was trouble there. She wanted me to keep an eye on her sister—she doesn't trust hotel security." He rolled his eyes. "When I mentioned that to Wasilick, it really made him mad," he added ruefully.

"I can believe that," Nancy said. "But look, maybe we can get Mr. Wasilick to call your girlfriend and have her verify your alibi. What's her name?"

"Bianca Fiorella," Paul said.

Chapter

Ten

BIANCA FIORELLA?" Nancy repeated, shocked. "You used to date Gina Fiorella's older sister?"

Paul glanced back at her. "You know Gina?"

"She was the girl you delivered the dead rat to last night!" Nancy told him.

He was stunned. "Wow," he murmured. "They don't look much alike, you know—Bianca's blond, and Gina's dark. But they both sure are knockouts."

"You never met Gina when you were dating Bianca?" Bess asked.

Paul shook his head. "Gina's boarding school isn't nearby, and the rest of the family lives in Rome," he explained. He winced. "I never met any of the family, in fact. They didn't approve of me. I guess they think a scholarship student who works as a waiter isn't good enough for Bianca."

"Why did you break up?" Nancy asked, curious.

Paul snorted. "Bianca's mom told her to stop seeing me—and she did. I never thought she'd be such a coward," he added bitterly. "But when Mrs. Fiorella cut off Bianca's allowance, she gave in. I'm better off without her," Paul said stiffly.

"But when she called last night, you ran over right away," George said. Nancy detected an edge of jealousy in her friend's voice.

Paul crossed his arms defensively. "I admit, I hoped she wanted us to get back together," he said. "But she was just using me to help out her family. As if I owed them anything!"

"Will Bianca support your alibi for last night?" Nancy asked Paul. He nodded.

"Would that convince Mr. Wasilick to give Paul his job back?" George asked Nancy.

"Possibly," Nancy said, "although Paul still did leave work when he wasn't supposed to. I can't really approach Mr. Wasilick about it. He doesn't like me. But I will try to talk to Ms. Peabody."

Paul broke into a relieved smile. "Thanks!" Waving goodbye, Paul climbed into his car and drove away. "I can't believe Mr. Wasilick suspects Paul of setting that fire," George said, annoyed.

"Well," Nancy said slowly, "he was missing at the right time. And if Mr. Wasilick knew Paul had a grudge against the Fiorellas—"

"Nancy, don't tell me *you* think Paul did anything wrong!" George interrupted, looking upset.

Nancy sighed. "He did deliver that dead rat, George," she said. "He fits Rosita's description of the man who lifted her passkey. He works in the kitchen, so he could have left those skewers. Maybe he does hate the Fiorellas, or maybe— what if Gina's dad's enemies paid him to get close to Bianca in the first place?"

George and Bess both drew back. "Nancy, you really have a suspicious mind," Bess said.

"Look, guys, I like Paul," Nancy insisted, "but we still don't know why this stuff is happening to Gina. The only way to prove Paul's innocence is to find out who really did these things. We have to step up our surveillance. Let's see . . . you both know what Jane Sellery looks like. But, George, you've never seen Nick Kessler. He's big and very muscular, with short dark hair, blue eyes, and a square jaw."

"Got it," George said. "I know what that guy with the beard looks like—I saw him yesterday at the pool."

"But I wouldn't be able to recognize him," Bess said. "Do you really consider him a suspect, Nancy?"

"It's just a hunch," Nancy said, "but we can't overlook anything. He could have heard us talking about the oleander, George. We know he was in the lobby two days ago, when Gina fell into the

91

pool." Suddenly Nancy paused. "Hey, Bess, he's in that photo Sally took of Evan Sharpless. Let's go see if she has a copy of it, to show you what he looks like. Even though her negatives were stolen, there's a chance she may have made some prints in the darkroom."

George said goodbye and headed for the pool, where she was scheduled to lifeguard. Nancy and Bess made their way to the workshop meeting area in the Muskoka Lobby. The red-carpeted landing was filled with students. Felt-covered blackboard-style displays had been set up in one section, and editors were busily pinning up photos, hand-lettered headlines, and typed squares of paper.

Nancy spotted Ned, leaning against a side wall. "There's Ned, so Gina must be nearby," Nancy said.

"There's Gina," Bess said, pointing to a blue display board with the school name Lloyd Hall mounted on it. Wielding a long steel ruler, Gina was intently lining up a photograph with a block of copy. Sally knelt at the bottom of the board, sorting through more photos. Both were dressed in George's old sweatsuits. Somehow, Nancy noticed, Gina still looked glamorous.

Sally saw Nancy and waved. Nancy walked over to admire the display. "Looks great," she said.

Gina leaned back, squinting critically. "I don't know why they stuck us in this dark corner," she complained. "Sally's pictures deserve better lighting, and nobody can read this copy I wrote."

"Gina, Sally, this is my friend Bess," Nancy said. "She works here at the hotel." Gina threw Bess a dismissive glance. Sally smiled and said hello.

"Bess is a big Evan Sharpless fan, Sally, and I told her you had some super shots of him," Nancy declared. "I hope they weren't all stolen."

"As a matter of fact," Sally said, "I'd just finished printing those pictures, so they were drying in the darkroom. They didn't get stolen with the stuff from our room. I've put them all up in this photo essay." She pointed to the display.

Bess leaned over to study the photos. The mystery man's face was mostly hidden behind his brown beard, and his build was hard to judge in the baggy khaki pants and army fatigue jacket he was wearing. Still, the picture gave Bess a good idea of his looks.

"Sharpless is so handsome," Bess said. "I really got excited when I saw him at the banquet yesterday. He was heroic, saving that boy's life."

"By the way, Gina," Nancy said casually. "I ran into a guy named Paul Lampedusa, who says he used to date your sister. Do you know him?"

Gina shrugged. "Nope," she said. "Now that Bianca's at college, I don't meet all her friends. And she has so many boyfriends—like all the Fiorella women." Nancy flinched and wondered if Gina counted Ned among them.

Just then Jane Sellery walked up. "Still using that vertical grid layout, Gina?" she asked snidely.

Gina flipped her dark hair back over her shoulder. "I don't believe in trendy layout styles," she said with a sniff. "But I guess they're handy when you have to disguise blurry photographs and badly written copy."

Jane looked scornfully at Gina. Sally leaned forward to interrupt them. "Look, Bess, there's your idol now," she said quickly, pointing across the room. Evan Sharpless was winding his way through the displays, stopping to talk to various editors.

"Show him your pictures," Bess suggested to Sally. "I'll bet he'll be flattered."

Sally squirmed modestly and tugged on a strand of her curly brown hair. "He'll love it, Sal," Gina urged. "TV people are always so vain. Mr. Sharpless?" Gina called to him.

The newscaster strolled over. "Mr. Sharpless, look at these great pictures of you that my coeditor took," Gina said. He leaned over and studied the photo essay briefly.

"Very nice," he commented blandly. "Good technique." Then, flashing a smile, he passed on. Sally looked hurt.

"See, Sal, I told you he's stuck-up," Gina said. "When I do that article for our school newspaper about our experiences at this conference, you can bet I'll expose what a shallow fraud that guy is."

"Oh, Gina, don't," Sally pleaded. "You can be so merciless in print." And in person, too, Nancy thought to herself.

Nancy and Bess soon left the girls to their work. Bess had to go back upstairs to put on her uniform to serve lunch. Nancy headed for Ms. Peabody's office to speak to her about Paul being fired.

As Nancy cut through the lobby, she saw Nick Kessler sitting on a bench by the elevators. He held an open newspaper, though he clearly wasn't reading it. Nancy paused, leaning on a nearby wall while she watched him covertly.

Just then Gina marched past, heading for the elevators, with Ned tagging behind. Nick Kessler held the paper in front of his face so they wouldn't notice him. Nancy ducked around a corner to hide.

Ping! An elevator arrived. Peeking around the corner, Nancy saw Ned and Gina step inside. Nick Kessler didn't move, but as soon as their elevator closed, he jumped up and ran over to push the Up button. Another elevator soon arrived, and he dashed inside.

Nancy scurried over as the elevator doors closed. She pushed the Up button urgently, hoping that the third elevator wasn't too far away.

It came almost at once. A middle-aged couple got off, tugging bulky suitcases behind them. Nancy squeezed past them into the car. Peering out the glass walls, she saw Ned and Gina's elevator glide to a stop above her. She swiftly counted upward. The elevator had stopped on seven.

She punched the button for seven. As her elevator climbed, Nancy noticed through the glass that Nick Kessler's car had also stopped on seven.

At the seventh floor Nancy hurried to an alcove in the corridor. She peered out and saw Gina and Ned at the door of Ned's old room, where Gina and Sally were staying now. Nick Kessler seemed to have vanished.

Nancy saw Ned open the door and step inside, probably to check the room, she thought. Gina waited in the hallway.

Then Nancy saw Nick's head poke out from the service corridor. Seeing Gina, he darted back. Why was he spying on her? Nancy wondered.

Ned came back out of the room and motioned to Gina to enter. Gina stepped past him, then abruptly stopped. Nancy saw her rise up on her toes, slip an arm around Ned's neck, and kiss him!

Nancy froze as she watched them intently. It sure looked to her as if Ned was kissing Gina back!

Nancy reeled back around the corner. She punched the elevator Down button, feeling sick. That's what I get for snooping on people, she thought wretchedly.

An Up elevator was just stopping. Someone

came up behind Nancy and ran for the elevator. She turned, expecting to see Nick Kessler.

It was the bearded man, dressed in the same baggy pants and fatigue jacket he was wearing in the photo! Seeing Nancy, the man looked scared. He rushed past Nancy and into the car. Before Nancy could act, the elevator doors closed and he was gone.

At least we know he's still in the hotel, Nancy thought. But why was he going up? Most guests usually travel between their own floor and the lobby. And if his room wasn't on seven, then why was he here?

Suddenly someone called out, "Miss?" Nancy turned to see Rosita, waving something in her hand—a passkey. "I found it!" Rosita exclaimed.

"Where?" Nancy asked, amazed.

"On the floor in my supply closet," Rosita said. "I must have dropped it there yesterday."

"But you searched your closet carefully yesterday," Nancy said. "Maybe whoever stole the key slipped it under the locked door this morning." Immediately she thought of the bearded man in the baggy pants. Was that why he was here just now?

Rosita frowned stubbornly. "But that nice man yesterday would not steal my key," she insisted.

"Maybe he found it in his room and returned it," Nancy said. "If you see him again, please let me know so we can thank him." Rosita nodded.

Hearing footsteps, Nancy looked past Rosita

and saw Gina and Ned coming down the corridor. Ned started guiltily when he saw Nancy. She flushed.

"Hello, Nancy," Gina said carelessly. "Anyway, Ned, let's get Sally and go shopping now. She went to lunch, but we can skip it. The food here is so awful anyway. There must be a decent restaurant near the stores. Where *are* the best clothing stores in River Heights?"

"Maybe Nancy can tell you," Ned suggested.

Gina swiveled and looked at Nancy's faded blue denim skirt and pink cotton T-shirt. "You know where the chic stores are?" she asked skeptically.

Nancy knitted her hands, yearning to put them around Gina's slender throat. Then she looked at Ned and saw a flicker of amusement in his eyes. I imagine there's a drop of humor in this situation, she thought, but I don't feel like searching for it now.

An elevator arrived, and the three stepped inside. Trying to sound friendly, Nancy told Gina about some good shops, conscious of Ned's eyes on them both.

Soon the elevator reached the main lobby, and the three made their way to the banquet room near the Muskoka Lobby. While Gina ran inside to get Sally, Nancy and Ned waited outside the door.

"Nancy," Ned said in a low voice, "you know you don't have anything to worry about."

Should I tell him I saw that kiss? Nancy

wondered. She began to open her mouth, but at that moment they heard shouts out by the escalators. Nancy and Ned raced to the landing and saw orange flames licking at the sides of one of the felt display boards.

Gina and Sally's display was on fire!

Chapter

Eleven

A MAINTENANCE MAN in green coveralls ran across the landing, calling over his shoulder for help. He had a fire extinguisher in his hand. When he reached Gina and Sally's display, he started to spray foam onto the burning felt board.

Ned rushed over to pull a fire alarm on a nearby wall. Nancy grabbed another extinguisher from the wall below the alarm and ran over to help put out the flames.

The smoke from the fire finally reached the smoke detectors in the landing ceiling. Sprinkler heads in the ceiling let off long sprays of water, and Nancy's hair and clothes were soon soaked. The fire dwindled to a wet sizzle.

When the River Heights firefighters arrived, three minutes later, the fire was already out. Lowering her fire extinguisher, Nancy sighed as she looked at what was left. The other students' displays were drenched but otherwise intact. Gina and Sally's display was a black, smoldering mess.

Ned had already gone to find Gina and Sally in the banquet room. As the circle of firefighters stood surveying the scene, Gina pushed past them. Her dark eyes flashed angrily. "This can't be an accident," she declared hotly. "I stayed up all night writing that copy, and now it's destroyed. Someone has done this on purpose, and I want to know who!"

Joining the crowd, Gary Ruxton looked anguished. "Who discovered the fire?" he demanded.

The maintenance worker who'd helped Nancy put out the fire raised his hand. He was a short, thickset man with curly black hair and a mustache.

"I was replacing some lightbulbs in the Riverview Ballroom," he said, pointing to the end of the landing. "When I came out, I heard fire crackling. At first I couldn't see where it was—there were too many displays in the way. But then the flames came shooting out. I found an extinguisher and ran over."

"Was anyone else in the area?" Nancy asked.

The worker shook his head. "No one," he said.

"Did any electrical items short out?" the fire captain asked. "Any sign of a dropped cigarette? What about the covers on these display boards—are they flammable?" The fire captain and Mr. Ruxton moved aside to discuss the fire. The other firefighters headed down the escalator, while a maintenance crew began to clean up.

Nancy turned to Sally and Gina. Sally's gray eyes welled up, and one fat tear rolled over her black lashes and onto her cheek. "Those were the only prints I had of those pictures," she moaned softly. "The negatives disappeared when our room was burned last night. I wanted to enter those shots in the photography competition. I'm sure they would have won a prize. But there's no way now."

Gina put an arm around Sally's shoulders. "I'm going to buy you a new camera right now," she said firmly. "Then you can take more pictures and you'll enter those in the contest. And you will win, I know it. Don't let these people get to you, Sally. That's what they *want*." She led her friend away.

"Gotta go," Ned said quickly to Nancy. "But look—we need to talk. After she takes Sally shopping, Gina will be in classes all afternoon. Can you meet me at the café at three?"

Nancy nodded listlessly. Ned lifted her chin with one finger and looked deep into her blue eyes. She had to smile. "See you at three," she promised.

As Ned hurried off, Nancy knelt to look closer at the area around the charred display. She had to agree with Gina—this was no accident. She sniffed the air for the telltale smells of gasoline or lighter fluid, sure signs of arson.

On the carpet at the base of the display, Nancy

spotted several blackened matches. The fire *had* been started intentionally!

Then, as she sat back on her heels, Nancy spied a neon orange matchbook lying on the carpet, five feet away. She reached over to pick it up. The cover was open, and every match inside had been torn out.

Closing the cover, she looked at the front of the sodden matchbook. Bold blue letters spelled out Ben's Back Room—Washington, D.C.

A clue at last! Nancy thought triumphantly. Clutching the matchbook, she hurried over to give her evidence to the fire chief.

As soon as Bess was off duty, Nancy and George met her by the pool. "Let's review our list of suspects," Nancy suggested. "The fire broke out at twelve-thirty, so it was probably set about twelve twenty-five. Where was Jane Sellery?"

"She was one of the first people in the banquet room at lunch today," Bess reported. "No way would she have been able to set that fire."

"Nick Kessler was in the hotel, and so was Mr. Baggy Pants," Nancy put in. "I didn't see them anywhere near that landing, it's true. But they might have had time to get there before me, if they took some other route from the seventh floor. Now that I think of it, the guy with the beard took the elevator to a higher floor when I saw him. He could have done that to throw me—and then he could have gone down again."

George drew a cautious breath. "And then

there's Paul," she volunteered. "He was near the hotel this morning, at least. How about if I call him and see whether he has an alibi between the time we saw him and twelve-thirty?"

Nancy nodded. "If we can clear him, all the better," she said. "I still think Nick Kessler and Mr. Baggy Pants are our strongest suspects. But it's pretty hard to tail them. We have no idea where they're staying."

"I'm not working again until six," Bess said. "I'll plant myself in the lobby and wait till one of them comes by. And by the way, Ralph told me this is his day off, so I'm safe from him today."

"That's great," Nancy said with a grin. "Whichever of those two guys you see, follow him, whether he's going in or out. I'll go talk to Gina. Maybe we can learn some more about Kessler."

Hurrying up to the seventh floor, Nancy hoped to catch Gina between shopping and her afternoon classes. Ned was outside the room on his folding chair. As Nancy knocked on the door, he tugged on her skirt and murmured, "Three o'clock—can't wait."

Nancy flipped him a quick smile as Sally opened the door. "Can I talk to Gina for a minute?" Nancy asked.

Gina, sitting on the bed beside a heap of shopping bags, waved to Nancy. "I'm glad you're here," she said. "These incidents are getting too serious. You have to find out who's behind it all."

"Tell me who you think it is," Nancy said, settling into an armchair.

"My dad's political enemies have often threatened to hurt me or my sister at home in Italy," Gina said. "That's why Daddy insists we each have a bodyguard. My mom's American, and she thinks we're safe if we go to school in this country. But what if the enemies have followed us here now?"

"Had Nick Kessler been with you long?" Nancy asked.

"Nick?" Gina said. "He'd only worked for me three weeks. He used to guard a friend of Daddy's—a man at the Italian embassy in Washington."

Nancy thought of the matchbook she'd found. It was from Washington, D.C. Had Nick Kessler dropped it while setting the display on fire?

"Did he have a keycard for your room?" Nancy asked. "Maybe he was the one who broke in."

Gina and Sally traded an uneasy look. "I made Nick return that card when I fired him," Gina said.

"Tell her, Gina," Sally said in a low voice. Her gentle gray eyes actually looked stern.

Nancy perked up. "Tell me what?"

Sally turned to Nancy. "Well," she began, "Gina faked the first break-in, hoping to make Jane Sellery look bad. Gina messed up our room herself and then put that Brookfield pen under the bed. She'd swiped it from Jane that afternoon. She told me the truth last night, after the fire, because I was so scared about all these incidents. I told her she had to tell you."

Nancy turned to Gina, stunned. "Why did you do that? Jane might have gotten into serious trouble."

Gina tossed her head and looked away. "It was a practical joke," she said. "I saw Jane laughing at me in the lobby after I fell in the water, and it made me angry. I wanted to get back at her."

Nancy blew out a sigh of disgust. "So just to carry on this stupid feud, you created all this trouble?" she asked angrily. "Do you realize that someone from the housekeeping staff nearly got fired because of that break-in? Not to mention the worry it caused Mr. Ruxton and Ms. Peabody and Mr. Wasilick—"

Gina stuck out her jaw. "I didn't expect people to take it so seriously," she said sullenly. "But then the other stuff happened, and *that* was real." She looked up at Nancy. "The person who was almost fired—is her job safe now?" she asked, sounding sincere.

"Well, yes, but she had a very unpleasant couple of days," Nancy said tensely. "Now I'm going to have to rethink my whole investigation. At least I can drop Jane from the suspect list." She drew an exasperated breath. "Will you both be at the workshop all afternoon?"

Gina and Sally nodded.

"I'll meet you here just before dinner," Nancy

said. "Tomorrow's the last day of the conference. Until then, Gina, be careful. This hotel is a prime place for our culprit to hurt you—I'll bet he strikes again before you leave. Be on your guard every minute!"

Saying goodbye to Gina and Sally, Nancy went down to the lobby. As she hunted for Bess, Nancy tried to get her mind off Gina's prank. Feeling a tap on her shoulder, she spun around quickly.

"It's me," Bess said with a cheerful grin. "Guess who I found? Mr. Baggy Pants."

"You did?" Nancy asked, her spirits rising.

Bess nodded. "He came in through the front doors and I followed him upstairs," she reported. "He went to room 637. He had a keycard and let himself in."

"Good work!" Nancy said with delight. "Sixth floor, huh? But he was on seven earlier today, and he took the elevator *up*—not back down to six. Seems pretty suspicious to me. The front desk won't give out information on guests, but maybe Ms. Peabody can help us find this guy's name. And while we're there, we can speak to her about Paul's job."

The girls went to Maureen Peabody's office. Ms. Peabody wasn't in, the secretary told them, but she had been authorized to give Nancy access to any information she needed. Her computer showed them that room 637 was registered to a Harold Karabell from Chicago.

At Nancy's request, the secretary agreed to make a printout of all the phone numbers that

Karabell had dialed from his room during his stay. It would be ready in an hour, she said.

"So he's from Chicago—that doesn't tie him to the Washington, D.C., matchbook I found," Nancy said as she and Bess left the office. "And there's still the possibility he's with the workshop. Can you find Mr. Ruxton and check out that angle?"

Bess nodded eagerly and sprinted off.

Looking at her watch, Nancy saw it was almost three. She hurried to the escalator and rode it up to the mezzanine-level café. Ned waved from a table.

Sitting down across from him, Nancy ordered an iced tea. As the waiter left, Ned pushed aside the small candleholder on the table and took Nancy's hands in his. "This whole thing has been crazy, Nan," he began. "I didn't realize bodyguarding was a twenty-four-hour-a-day job. Here we are, both staying in the same hotel, and we can't spend any time together. Thank goodness this job ends when the conference is over."

"Whenever we *do* see each other, Gina always pops up," Nancy added. "She really has her eye on you."

Ned made a face. "Yeah," he said. "At first I thought it was kind of fun. You know, it's flattering to have a girl throw herself at you, especially a girl that pretty. But she comes on *too* strong. It's like she wants to own me. I hate that."

"And I hate being jealous," Nancy said with a sigh. "I know I don't own you, Ned, and I don't want to. But it hurts to see you with someone else."

"I'm not 'with' her," Ned said firmly. "Nancy, why would I dump you for Gina? You're prettier, you're smarter, you're nicer—" Leaning over the table, he gently brushed her lips with his.

A moment later, they pulled away from the kiss and smiled at each other. Nancy glanced past Ned for a second. Then she sat up, alert.

The bearded man with the baggy pants was at the next table. Harold Karabell!

Karabell was nervously fiddling with the small candle on his table. As he tipped it to the side, melted wax spilled over, snuffing out the wick. Frowning, he fished a matchbook out of his roomy pants pockets and relit the candle.

Peering over Ned's shoulder, Nancy stared at the matchbook. It was neon orange, with bold blue letters on the side. Ben's Back Room, it read.

A perfect match!

Chapter

Twelve

Ned looked at Nancy, concern in his eyes. "What is it, Nan? What do you see?"

"Don't turn around, Ned," she murmured. "But the guy at the table behind you is one of my suspects. In fact, I think he's just become my prime suspect."

The waiter bringing Ned's and Nancy's drinks approached the table. Karabell's gaze idly followed the waiter. When he saw Nancy, he panicked. He jumped up at once and headed out of the café area.

"He's leaving, Ned!" Nancy said. "I've got to follow him. Wait here." She scrambled to her feet and sprinted to the escalator.

Nancy spotted Karabell farther down the escalator, taking the moving steps two at a time. In front of Nancy, two men in business suits took up the whole width of the escalator. She couldn't squeeze past them. "Excuse me," she said impatiently.

Deep in a discussion, the men seemed not to hear her. They didn't move. Nancy asked again, and once more the men ignored her.

Nancy fidgeted as the escalator descended at its own snail's pace. She leaned over, trying to keep an eye on Karabell. She saw him hustle off the foot of the escalator and run for the front entrance.

Springing off the escalator, Nancy dodged around the two businessmen and dashed through the lobby. She slid into a revolving door and shoved it around as fast as she could. She burst out into the hot, humid summer air. After being in the air-conditioned hotel nonstop for two days, she was surprised to remember what real air felt like.

Standing on the curb of the driveway, Nancy looked in all directions for Harold Karabell. A red-uniformed bellman stepped over to her. "Can I get you a taxi?" he asked.

"No, thanks," Nancy said. "But did you see a man with a brown beard come out just now? He was wearing baggy khaki pants and a green army jacket."

The bellman looked vague. "Yeah, he got into a cab," he said slowly. "There was one sitting here waiting for a fare, and he took it. It was a blue-and-white cab, I think—or maybe black-and-white."

That's not much help, Nancy thought. "Did

you happen to hear where he told it to go?" she asked. The bellman shook his head.

Discouraged, Nancy went back into the atrium. Rejoining Ned in the café, she briefly told him what had happened. "I saw he had a matchbook from a place in Washington, D.C.," she went on. "It was just like one that I found near Gina's display after the fire today. Considering how far we are from Washington, that's a pretty big coincidence."

"Who is this guy?" Ned asked.

"I don't really know," Nancy admitted. "But whenever I see him around the hotel, he always looks scared and runs away. I only know that he might be a friend of Evan Sharpless. Remember the first day of the workshop, when we saw Mr. Sharpless go up the escalator? This is the guy who talked to him then."

"Did you ask Mr. Sharpless who he is?" Ned asked.

"No, but I will now," she replied. "I didn't learn his name until just a few minutes ago."

"What is his name?" Ned asked. "I could ask Gina if she recognizes it. Since he seems to be after her, maybe she knows him."

"His name's Harold Karabell," Nancy told him. "Go ahead and ask her. But if he's been hired by her dad's enemies, they wouldn't use someone she knows. That's why it's so hard for the police to find hired killers. They have no connection to their victims."

"Hired killers?" Ned repeated, his eyes widening. "So, you really think someone is trying to kill Gina?"

"Maybe. Or kidnap her," Nancy said. "I do think this is more than just harassment."

"But the fire last night—and the one today— were planned for when she *wasn't* around," Ned pointed out. "If someone wanted to hurt her, why do it that way? And she wasn't there either time her room was broken into."

"Her room was only broken into once," Nancy said. She told him about Gina faking the first incident.

Ned chuckled at the story. "You have to admit, life around Gina is always interesting," he said.

"I don't mind it being interesting from a detective's point of view," Nancy said. "But from a personal point of view, I don't need the kind of interest Gina stirs up."

Ned smiled. "I told you, Nancy—you have nothing to worry about," he assured her. "But it's kind of cool to see that spark of jealousy in your eyes. Makes me feel I'm still wanted."

"Oh, you're still wanted, all right, Nickerson," Nancy said with a grin. They held hands tightly across the table as Ned called for their check. It feels good to clear the air, Nancy thought to herself. But who knows how I'll feel when I see Gina hanging all over him again? The memory of seeing Ned kissing Gina was still clear in her mind.

Leaving the café, Ned headed for the meeting rooms to wait for Gina's workshop to end. Nancy went to Ms. Peabody's office to pick up the printout of Harold Karabell's phone calls.

Taking the printout back to her room, Nancy looked first for any calls to Rome or Washington, D.C. But Karabell hadn't been on the phone much, and most of the calls were local. Nancy picked up her phone and began to dial each number listed.

The first one turned out to be a recorded message, giving show times for a nearby movie theater. The next number was a local bookstore.

The third number had a Chicago area code. Probably Karabell's home, Nancy assumed as she dialed. Then a voice answered, *"Chicago Post,* newsroom. Paula Rackow speaking."

Nancy cleared her throat. "Oh, hi, my name is Nancy Drew," she said. "I was wondering if you know a Harold Karabell."

"Harold? Sure," the journalist answered. "He and I worked together for a newswire service in Israel, four years ago. Why do you ask?"

"Have you heard from him lately?" Nancy asked.

"Who are you?" the reporter countered.

"I'm a private detective," Nancy said, "and someone has been harassing a client of mine. Mr. Karabell was seen near the scene of several incidents, so I'm checking him out."

The reporter laughed. "He's probably just snooping around for a story," she said. "Though I thought Harold's specialty was politics. Is your client a sleazy politician, by any chance? That would attract Harold's nose for news."

"Politics might be involved," Nancy said cautiously. "Do you know where he is?"

"He called me yesterday from River Heights," Ms. Rackow said. "But he just called to apologize for missing my housewarming party. He said he'd been called away unexpectedly. I thought he might be on a story, but he said he wasn't." She sounded concerned. "He hasn't worked much, you know, since he lost his job on the wire service. The last story of his I remember seeing was two years ago—something about a political assassination in Rome."

Rome! Nancy's heartbeat quickened. "Why did he lose his job on the wire service?" she asked.

Ms. Rackow sighed. "Who knows?" she said. "He's bright, witty, resourceful. He could always dig up hot leads. Sometimes he relied too much on informers, though. You know, shady anonymous sources. Harold liked the clandestine part of reporting. I used to kid him that he should have been a spy instead."

The reporter drew a breath and went on. "To tell the truth, he's not a very good writer," she said. "And he was never careful about verifying information. He wrote a couple of stories that were more hearsay than fact. It wasn't a very responsible thing to do."

"But you don't think he's the kind of guy who might harass someone?" Nancy asked.

"Not really," Ms. Rackow said. "He's too idealistic to stoop that low."

Thanking her, Nancy hung up. She sat on her bed, digesting the information. Karabell was a reporter—that would explain the Evan Sharpless connection. Was he following Gina as part of a story? Or were his contacts from Rome using him to go after Gina?

Over dinner in the employee cafeteria, George told Nancy and Bess what she had heard from Paul. "He has a pretty solid alibi," she said. "He was at the college, in the dining hall, working at his second job as a dish washer. I called the dining commons manager, and she vouched for him."

Nancy appreciated how careful George had been not to take Paul's word at face value. "I'm glad he checks out," she said. She speared a tomato from her salad. "And by the way, Jane Sellery's off the hook. It turns out Gina framed her for the break-in."

"Ooh, that little witch!" Bess exclaimed.

"I've got lots more on Mr. Baggy Pants," Nancy said, and she filled them in. "I guess he's our top suspect now."

"Gary Ruxton said he'd never heard of Karabell," Bess reported, buttering a baked potato.

"But Nick Kessler is still hanging around the hotel," George put in. "You know that picture window across from the pool, where you can see everyone on the weight machines in the health club? I looked in and saw Nick Kessler working out. So I went in and asked him why he's still here."

"George, you blew your cover!" exclaimed Nancy.

"He never saw me lifeguarding," George argued. "Besides, he's too dumb to figure it out. Anyway, he told me he's still here because he wants to keep an eye on Gina. He seemed genuinely concerned about her safety. I almost felt sorry for him—he did lose his job, after all. But he isn't mad at Gina, only at Ned."

"Where was he around noon today?" Nancy asked.

"He said he was out running. I guess there's no way to check that," George said. "But I asked him if he'd ever been to Ben's Back Room in Washington. He looked offended and said he never goes to bars. He doesn't ever drink, because his body is a temple." George raised her eyebrows. "Direct quote."

The girls cleared away their dinner trays, and George and Bess headed for the banquet room. Nancy went upstairs to check in with Gina, as promised.

As Nancy turned into the corridor on the seventh floor, she saw Gina and Sally ahead, waiting by their room door. Ned was just slipping the keycard into the door slot. Nancy jogged down the hall to join them.

As she drew closer, Nancy saw that Ned had stopped just inside the door. Bending down, he picked up an envelope that must have been slipped under the door. "You want to see what it is?" he asked Gina uncertainly.

Gina took the envelope from him and briskly broke it open. Nancy watched as Gina removed a sheet of hotel stationery, with a typewritten message.

From her position, Nancy observed that the note had the same typeface as the note sent to the chef with the shish kebab skewers. She glanced up to ask Gina if she could take this note to compare them.

But before she could speak, Nancy took in Gina's wide-eyed, trembling look. Gina was staring straight at Sally, her hands shaking.

Taking the note, Nancy read it quickly:

Don't take any more photos. Next time, you may be the one to be set on fire.

Nancy knew what Gina must be thinking. The threat wasn't meant for Gina at all.

It was meant for Sally!

Chapter

Thirteen

LET'S GO INSIDE the room," Nancy said to the girls quietly. As they all stepped inside, she firmly shut the door behind them.

Gina and Sally sat down meekly on their beds. Ned perched on the edge of a nearby desk. "Sally," Nancy said in an even voice, trying not to alarm her. "We've all been assuming that Gina is the target of these incidents. But could someone possibly be trying to harass *you?*"

Sally, looking shocked, began to twirl her hair nervously around a finger. "Me?" she said. "Why would anyone harass me? I'm just an ordinary high school kid."

"The note specifically calls attention to the photos in the display, *your* photos," Nancy pointed out. "Let's consider the other incidents. The first break-in, we know, was a hoax. But what about the second one? Nothing was taken.

The room wasn't even messed up. What could the thief have wanted?"

Sally squirmed. "Gina's jewelry wasn't touched," she said. "My only valuable was my camera, but I had it with me that morning. It wasn't in the room."

Nancy nodded, her mind racing. "Suppose the intruder wanted your camera," she said, talking out the case. "He would've realized then that you always have it with you. It's possible, then, that the dead rat in the pasta was a way to scare you out of your room."

"After the rat appeared, we went to the café," Ned recalled. "But you took your camera, Sally."

"Ralph, the bellman who was guarding your room then, did tell me that a man dressed as a maintenance worker tried to get in your room then," Nancy said. "Maybe he was looking for your camera. Luckily, Ralph wouldn't let him in."

"I did leave my camera in the room when the fire alarm went off," Sally said. "When I came back, it was gone. But Gina's clothes were ruined, too."

"I'll bet our culprit burned Gina's clothes as a diversion, so we'd still think she was the target," Nancy said.

Gina shivered. "We mounted the prints of Sally's photos on the display," she said. "Next thing we knew, it went up in flames." She frowned. "But what about the poisonous shish kebabs?"

"I haven't figured out that part yet," Nancy admitted. "It's hard to imagine that anyone would go to all that trouble for the slight chance that Sally would choose a shish kebab out of that big buffet."

"Except that I love shish kebabs," Sally said quietly. "And I had said so at lunch that day. We were sitting around talking about Middle Eastern food."

"Who was there when you said that?" Nancy asked.

Sally thought for a moment. "Mr. Ruxton and Mr. Sharpless were there—and Jane Sellery and her roommate, Karen. The boy who got sick that night was there, too. I forget his name, but Jane knows him."

"What about the very first day of the conference, when Gina was knocked into the water?" Ned asked.

"I had just been taking a picture of Sally," Gina said. "The camera was in my hand. It was knocked into the water with me."

"And I had been taking pictures with it a few minutes earlier," Sally added. "I was finishing off the roll of film I'd started in Florida."

An image popped into Nancy's mind, and she snapped her fingers. Of course—the photos of Harold Karabell with Evan Sharpless!

"I think I know who may be behind all this," she said tersely. "A journalist named Harold Karabell. Remember the bearded guy in the picture with Mr. Sharpless? That's him."

"Karabell?" Gina asked. She turned to Ned. "You just asked me if I knew him."

Ned nodded. "Nancy told me he was one of her suspects," he explained. "You didn't recognize the name, but that doesn't matter now. What matters is why he wanted the pictures Sally took of him destroyed."

Sally winced. "Whatever his reason, he's gotten his way," she said. "He stole the negatives and he burned up all my prints. The pictures are gone for good. If we can't look at them, we'll never know what it was he wanted to hide."

"Well, if they're gone for good, maybe all this trouble will stop," Ned said. "Let's hope so."

But Gina's eyes flashed. "How dare he go after my friend?" she declared. "He must be punished. Two fires, the shish kebabs—someone could have been badly hurt. Nancy, we need you now more than ever. You must catch this Harold Karabell!"

"I'll do my best," Nancy said gravely.

After a sleepless night, Nancy had a hard time getting up the next morning. Bess, scheduled for the breakfast shift in the banquet room, was long gone when Nancy finally sat up groggily. George was just putting on her lifeguard suit. "Call room service and order some breakfast," she advised Nancy.

"No, thanks," Nancy said, yawning. "Seeing that dead rat the other night really put me off room service."

George laughed. "Well, you've missed the breakfast downstairs," she said. "Make sure you stop by the snack table. What's on your agenda for today?" The night before, Nancy had told George and Bess about the startling new twist in the case. They had agreed that their top priority now should be finding as much proof as possible to link Harold Karabell to the crimes.

Nancy stretched her limbs. "I guess I'll go try to grill Harold Karabell," she said. "If we can learn what he's trying to cover up, maybe he'll confess to destroying Sally's pictures. He usually runs when he sees me coming, but it's worth a try."

"Did you talk to Ms. Peabody about getting Paul his job back?" George asked.

"No," Nancy said. "I'm sorry, George, but Ms. Peabody wasn't in yesterday when I went to her office, and then it slipped my mind. I promise I'll do it today."

But after George left, Nancy drifted back to sleep. She was awakened by the ringing of the phone. She answered it sleepily.

"Sally wants you to meet her in the workshop darkroom right away," Ned's voice said excitedly. "She's just found something that she thinks might give us the break we need."

Nancy was already out of bed. "Give me five minutes," she said eagerly. "Thanks, Ned. 'Bye!" She bounded over to the closet and pulled a navy-and-white-checked T-shirt dress off a hanger. Dressing in record time, she was out the door in minutes.

Nancy made her way to the Muskoka Lobby. Grabbing a muffin from the snack table, she ran into the meeting room where the photography classes were being held. The door of the darkroom was ajar. "Sally?" she called, peeking in.

"Nancy?" Sally's voice rose. "Come on in."

Inside the darkroom, Sally triumphantly held up a sheet of photographic paper. Nancy saw what looked like dozens of miniature photographs.

"My contact sheet!" Sally announced. "This morning I remembered I'd left it here. It's a quick one-sheet print of all the pictures on one roll of film. A photographer looks at a contact sheet to decide which individual shots to print. That way, you print only the pictures you really want."

"Does it have the pictures of Karabell on it?" Nancy asked breathlessly.

"Every last one of them!" Sally declared.

The girls went out to a table in the meeting room to study the contact sheet. Half a dozen other students were busy with various projects, but Sally and Nancy were too excited to notice them.

Sally picked up a small circular magnifying glass. Tucking her curly hair behind her ears, she bent over the tiny images. "It was a thirty-six-exposure roll of film, and I'd shot only five pictures on it in Florida," she recalled. "So I was just snapping away that afternoon. That's the only way to get a really good candid shot. It looks like I've got thirty or so shots here. Look." She handed the magnifying loupe to Nancy.

Nancy studied the sequence of photographs. She could see Evan Sharpless waving to the students and stepping onto the escalator. In four successive shots, he moved steadily up the escalator, looking all around. Then he stepped off at the mezzanine-level café and Harold Karabell entered the picture.

"They're not all great photos, artistically speaking," Sally said. "That's why I printed only five of them. Only one shot I printed had Karabell in it. Once Mr. Sharpless got to the mezzanine, he was too far away for me to get much, even with my telephoto lens. But there are several more shots on the contact sheet. Do you really think they might hold a clue?"

Nancy peered intently at the sequence of images through the magnifying glass. She could see Evan Sharpless looking over his shoulder— nervously, she thought. In the next shot, he pulled a thick envelope out of his suit pocket. In the shot after that, he handed the envelope to Karabell.

In the next shot, Karabell was looking inside the envelope, while Sharpless looked anxiously behind him.

And in the next shot, Karabell pulled a thick wad of money out of the envelope!

Chapter

Fourteen

SALLY AND NANCY stared at the photos in uneasy silence. "Why would Evan Sharpless be giving this Karabell guy so much money?" Sally finally asked.

Nancy swallowed hard. "There could be lots of reasons," she said, speculating. "A gambling debt, a blackmail payment, a payoff for an informant. A *Chicago Post* editor I talked to said Karabell often depends on secret sources for his stories. Maybe Mr. Sharpless needed to use one of Karabell's sources, and Karabell was the middle man."

"Or maybe it's like Gina said the other day," Sally put in. "Maybe Mr. Sharpless paid off the judges to award him the Hazelden prize."

Nancy looked skeptical. "I really don't think its judges would take bribes," she said. "They're very well-known journalists. And from what I learned, I doubt Karabell would be a Hazelden judge.

"Let's go back to the idea that it's a blackmail payment," Nancy continued, looking over her shoulder. Suddenly she was very aware of not letting the others in the room overhear their conversation.

"Karabell apparently is the sort of journalist who's good at digging up dirt on people," she went on quietly. "Maybe he dug up something on Evan Sharpless and then asked him for money in exchange for keeping quiet. The word is that Karabell's career hasn't been going so well lately. Maybe he needed the money."

Sally frowned. "That's blackmail."

"Exactly," Nancy replied. "That's why Karabell doesn't want those pictures around. He could be arrested for extortion. That's a serious charge."

Sally looked down, awed, at her contact sheet. "What do we do next, Nancy?" she asked.

"I think we should go to Ms. Peabody, the general manager, and ask her to call in the police," Nancy suggested. "They can interrogate Karabell and get to the bottom of this case." She glanced at the tiny images on the sheet. "Too bad those pictures are so hard to look at. If we want to force a confession, it would be more effective to have big, clear photos."

"I can't enlarge them very easily without the

original negatives," Sally said. "But we could use an opaque projector to show them on a wall or something. Mr. Ruxton may have some ideas."

"Great," Nancy said. "Find Mr. Ruxton and tell him what happened—show him the contact sheet and everything. Then see if you can get the enlarger. Meanwhile, I'll try to track down Karabell."

Leaving the meeting room, Nancy hurried straight for Maureen Peabody's office. The secretary there told Nancy that the general manager was in the Riverview Lounge. The new rooftop lounge was to be opened at a gala Saturday night, she said, and Ms. Peabody was checking out the last details. She added that the elevators had been programmed not to go up there yet, but Nancy could take the elevator to twelve and walk one flight up the fire stairs.

Following the secretary's directions, Nancy soon found herself walking out into a circular restaurant, with windows on all sides. The views of River Heights were spectacular. The tables nearest the windows were set on a lower level, giving the center tables a full panorama. Soft carpeting and upholstered chairs set an elegant tone.

Maureen Peabody was standing by the windows with two men in suits. Seeing Nancy, she excused herself and came over. Nancy quickly told her what she and Sally had found. "We think this man may be extorting hush money from

Evan Sharpless," Nancy said. "He probably broke into Sally's room and set both of the fires. He may even have been responsible for those deadly skewers at the banquet the night before last. I'd like to call in the police."

Ms. Peabody frowned. "You have very little evidence on which to arrest somebody," she pointed out.

"I'm not asking for him to be arrested—just to be brought in for questioning," Nancy said. "If he's innocent, he should be glad to help us."

Reluctantly, Ms. Peabody walked over to a phone and called the police. Then Nancy and Ms. Peabody hurried down to the lobby to meet them. Ten minutes later, they accompanied two police detectives to the sixth floor and hammered on Karabell's door. There was no answer. "We can't spend all day waiting around for a guy who *might* be responsible for two tiny fires and a couple of small break-ins," one of the police detectives told Nancy.

"But he might also be a blackmailer," Nancy said.

"You've got no proof of that yet," the detective answered. "Call us when you do." The two men headed back downstairs.

Frustrated, Nancy went back down with Ms. Peabody to her office. "Maybe I could look on the billing computer and see if he made any more phone calls," Nancy suggested, standing by the manager's desk. "That might explain what he's still doing here. After all, Bess and I both saw him yesterday *after* the display burned. There must be a reason why he's hanging around."

"Fine with me," Ms. Peabody said.

Her secretary called up Karabell's name on the computer. "Room 637?" she said. "He checked out at eight-fifteen this morning."

Seething with frustration, Nancy trudged back up to the banquet room, where she grabbed a roast beef sandwich. Nancy asked Bess, who was waiting tables, to look out for Sally and tell her that Karabell had checked out. Then Nancy went to the darkroom, looking for Sally, but she wasn't there.

Next Nancy stopped by the pool. Sitting dejectedly in a deck chair, she told George about the morning's discoveries. When she got to the part about Karabell checking out this morning, George sat up in her chair.

"Eight-fifteen?" she repeated. "Nancy, he was here at the pool this morning. It was around eleven o'clock, long after he'd checked out."

Nancy stared at George, amazed. "Are you sure?"

George nodded. "Positive."

"Then he *is* hanging around for some reason," Nancy said excitedly. "Maybe we can still catch him!"

At six o'clock Nancy returned to her room, disappointed again. She had spent the afternoon hunting for Karabell. Armed with a layout of the hotel, she'd posted people at every strategic point—Bess at a side door just off the Muskoka Lobby, Ned in the meeting area, George at the employees' entrance down in the basement, Stan Wasilick in the underground parking garage, and Ralph at the front entrance. She'd even convinced Ms. Peabody to offer Paul his job back and ask him to cover the loading docks where trucks delivered supplies.

With Ms. Peabody's help, Sally had used the office copier to enlarge the best shot of Karabell from her contact sheet. That way, Nancy was able to show a usable picture to each of the people on guard. Then Nancy had stationed herself in the lobby, next to a house phone, so that her various pairs of "eyes" could contact her.

But by five o'clock, when the student editors came flocking back through the lobby, heading for their rooms, there had been no sign of Karabell. Reluctantly, Nancy headed upstairs to dress for the final banquet. Evan Sharpless would be giving his keynote speech there, and the newscaster might be the reason Karabell had lingered at the hotel. It's our last hope, Nancy thought dejectedly.

As she slipped into a hot-pink linen dress with a flared skirt, Nancy wondered wearily if Karabell wasn't already long gone. She had his address in Chicago, but she doubted that the Chicago police would be willing to call him in for questioning. After all, the River Heights police hadn't seemed interested in the case.

Standing before a mirror, she pulled a brush through her reddish blond hair. I guess I could have put more effort into my appearance, she thought. Gina's sure to be dressed to kill. But time was running out. If Karabell showed up at the banquet, she had to be there, not in the shower. Ned would understand, she decided.

As she stepped into the hallway, Rosita Ortiz came bustling up. "Miss, you ask me to tell you when I saw the man who had me use my pass-key," Rosita said breathlessly. "I saw him leave a room on the ninth floor. I followed him. He went into the big room where the students have dinner."

Nancy tensed up. "The Riverview Ballroom?" she checked. "Up the escalator from the Muskoka Lobby?"

Rosita nodded. "He is wearing a gray coat and pants, and a—" She pantomimed knotting a tie with her hands.

"A necktie," Nancy said. "That's great, Rosita, thanks!" She rushed down the corridor, eager to follow the lead. Karabell was still here!

Nancy hurried from the elevator to the Muskoka Lobby and strode swiftly up the escalator steps. She dashed into the ballroom and began to look around for a man in a gray suit.

She saw Gina and Sally, seated at a table near the podium, with Ned standing against the nearest wall. Nancy crossed over to them and told

Ned to watch for Karabell, who was wearing a gray suit. Ned nodded and started to prowl the perimeter of the ballroom.

Just then Gary Ruxton stepped up to the podium. "Good evening," he said. "While you're eating, we'd like to show you some of the entries in this year's photography contest. We've had some fine work this year." He stepped aside as a machine projected the first picture onto a screen behind a long front table. It was a soft-focus shot of a boy playing a guitar.

Nancy spotted Evan Sharpless at the end of the front table. Paul was at his shoulder, handing him his dinner plate. Then Nancy froze.

Evan Sharpless was wearing a gray suit and a necktie!

So it was Sharpless who had "borrowed" Rosita's passkey! Everything clicked into place in Nancy's mind. Sharpless could have had as much reason to destroy Sally's photos as Karabell had. If Karabell was blackmailing him, there must be some terrible secret the newscaster wanted to hide. He certainly didn't seem like a man who would stoop to crime to protect himself, but what if that was all a cunning facade?

Nancy shifted her gaze to the screen. There, enlarged against the wall, was a picture from Sally's contact sheet, showing Sharpless going up the escalator! Nancy prayed he wouldn't see it. But as a murmur of recognition rose from the crowd, he looked up, twisted his head around, and saw himself onscreen.

Nancy, acting on instinct, started across the ballroom toward Sharpless. Ned, on the far side of the room, began to move, too. But Sharpless had already sprung from his seat and was lunging for Sally. Everyone in the room turned toward the commotion.

Grabbing Sally by the arm, Sharpless tore her from her chair and jerked her over to the doors leading to the pantry. He held Sally in front of him, a gun pointed at her head.

"No one had better stop me!" he shouted wildly. Then he spun around, shoved Sally through the doorway, and followed her out of sight.

Chapter

Fifteen

GINA LET OUT a blood-curdling scream as she saw her roommate disappear at gunpoint. Ned ran to her side. Gary Ruxton leapt to the podium, trying to control the uproar that had broken out in the ballroom.

Nancy sprinted over to the pantry doors. Peering through a small round window in one door, she saw that Sharpless and Sally were already gone. The only way out of the pantry was by way of the service elevator, she knew. She ducked into the pantry, picked up the house phone, and called the kitchen.

The phone rang several times. A breathless male voice finally answered. "I'm calling from the Riverview Ballroom on three," Nancy said quickly.

"Is that Nancy?" the voice answered. "It's me, Paul. What's up?"

"Oh, Paul!" Nancy exclaimed. "I'm so glad it's you. Look, Evan Sharpless has just abducted Sally Harvey. He dragged her into the pantry up here, but now I can't find them. They must have gotten into the elevator. Have they reached the kitchen yet?"

"No," Paul said. "But I can see the numbers lit up above the elevator. It's not coming down here—it's going up. It's stopped at twelve."

Twelve? Nancy thought. Why would Sharpless take Sally to the twelfth floor? What was there?

Then she remembered the Riverview Lounge. One floor up from twelve—a part of the hotel no other guests would go to, where no staff had any business. What better place to take a hostage!

"Paul, you stay by that elevator. If Sharpless comes down, don't let him off!" Nancy ordered. "I'm going up to the rooftop lounge to try to find him." Hanging up, she dashed back into the ballroom.

As she sprinted around the tables, she saw Ned talking on another house phone near the doors. He waved to her and called, "I've got Peabody. She's calling the cops!"

Nancy nodded, grateful for Ned's quick thinking. "Have them cover all the exits and send some up to the rooftop lounge!" she shouted. Then she ran out the door.

Nancy ran hard through the empty meeting area, catapulted down the escalator, and tore off through the Muskoka Lobby and down to the main lobby. Crowds of people milled about: new guests arriving, other guests leaving the hotel for dinner, and diners coming to eat at the hotel's restaurants.

Nancy pushed impatiently through the crowds to the elevator bank. An Up elevator was just closing. Nancy flung herself through the doors just in time.

The other guests in the elevator stared at Nancy. As she fought to catch her breath, she tried to look nonchalant, smoothing back her hair. There was no point in alarming the guests, she realized.

Nancy pressed the button for the twelfth floor, noticing that buttons for several floors had already been pushed. She was in for a slow ride with many stops. She only hoped Sally would be safe until she got to her!

No one else was left on the elevator when Nancy reached the twelfth floor. She jumped off and raced to the fire stairs she'd gone up earlier. Climbing the stairs, she tried to be as quiet as possible. She didn't want to scare Sharpless unnecessarily, not while he held that gun.

As she neared the top, she heard voices arguing —two male voices. She pushed the door at the top open ever so gently. Cautiously, she peeked around it.

Sharpless was standing near the window. River Heights was spread out behind him, glowing as the sun began to set. With his left hand clamped around Sally's upper arm, he held the revolver in his right hand, close to her temple. The barrel of the gun nestled into her soft brown curls. Sally's face looked gray with terror.

Facing them, a few yards away, stood Harold Karabell, in his old baggy khakis.

"Contribution, you call it!" Karabell shouted at Sharpless. "That wasn't just background research I did for you. I gave you entire stories—facts, figures, quotes, the whole works. All you did was rewrite them a little, in your fancy hotel rooms. Then you'd go on the air, reading them as though you'd dug them all up yourself. You are a fraud."

Sharpless twitched angrily, giving Sally's arm an inadvertent yank. "And you were paid for your work," he snarled.

"Paid?" Karabell said. "That money wasn't even a fraction of what your salary was. But I wasn't in it just for the money. You said you'd give me credit, help me find another job. You never did. My name never appeared in the credits at the end of the newscast. You never mentioned me in your big bestselling book—even though I wrote half of it for you. You got paid thousands of dollars for speeches about the stories I covered for you, and I can't even make my mortgage payments."

"You should be glad I even gave you work, after you printed those false rumors in Rome," Sharpless retorted. "No one else would hire you then."

"Where do you come off, acting so righteous?" Karabell said hotly. "I published that story in good faith. It's not my fault those rumors were false. But that's nothing compared to what you did. Your famous interview with the guerrilla leader in Afghanistan—you made the whole thing up, from start to finish. There never even *was* such a man. And then you won the Hazelden Prize for it!"

"Look, I paid you to shut up about that," Sharpless said angrily.

"You can't even be honest about that," Karabell replied. "You said you'd give me five thousand dollars, but you gave me only two thousand. I knew I should have stopped to count it on the mezzanine the other day."

Sharpless uttered a short, nasty laugh. "So what are you going to do, go to the cops?" he scoffed. "You accepted money. That makes you a blackmailer. And the way you've been dogging me the past few days, I could probably sue you for harassment, too. Expose me now, and you go to jail."

"That whole room of kids downstairs has seen the pictures," Karabell said in a leaden voice. "You might as well give up. You're ruined. We both are."

"How do we know?" Sharpless answered. Nancy, listening at the door, thought his voice sounded higher than usual, and strained. "Maybe they won't figure out what's going on in those photos."

"Maybe not, but they sure did see you abduct the girl," Karabell said. "With a gun, too. So stupid. I suspected you were going off the deep end a while ago, Evan, but I never thought you'd turn to violence."

Sharpless waved his gun in the air with a loony little laugh. Nancy saw Sally shiver with fear. "You know why I brought this gun to River Heights?" he said. "I was thinking of shooting *you*, Harold." He swung the gun around to point it at Karabell. "That would be a lot cheaper than paying you off, and more permanent, too."

"Shoot me, shoot the girl—then you'll be facing a murder rap," Karabell said in an oddly calm voice. "And that's a whole lot worse than a plagiarism charge. I wouldn't take the chance."

Sharpless snorted. "Murder rap?" he said. "Who knows if they could make it stick. I've been pretty crafty so far, haven't I? I went into action as soon as I saw this little snoop with her camera." He gave Sally's arm a particularly vicious tug.

"No one saw me go back down to the lobby and push the trolley to knock her camera into the water," he went on, bragging. "No one knew I got that passkey to break into her room. No one knew I tried to poison everyone at the banquet. They all thought I was a hero for saving that one boy!"

"You tried to poison all those innocent kids?" Karabell asked, horrified.

"Oh, I wouldn't have let anyone die," Sharpless said. "I knew how to save their lives. But I figured if they all got sick, the conference would be cancelled and she'd go home—away from you, Harold. I figured only you could tell her what was going on in those photos."

"You really are paranoid," Karabell said. "All this fuss just to get rid of a few shots . . ."

"Well, I got rid of them, didn't I?" Sharpless claimed. "I got to know this hotel inside out. I even dressed up as one of the maintenance crew. What better way to make myself invisible! I finally had to pull a fire alarm, but I got those negatives. And then another little blaze took care of the prints."

"If you got rid of them, then why were they shown at the banquet downstairs just now?" Karabell said. "When I looked through the doors and saw them, I thought I'd have a heart attack."

Sharpless turned to Sally, yanking fiercely on her arm. "I don't know. Where did they come from?" he demanded. "You little sneak."

Sally's mouth opened and closed soundlessly. Nancy guessed she was too terrified to speak.

Suddenly the elevator bell rang. *Ping!* The police, Nancy thought with relief. Ms. Peabody must have had someone reprogram the elevators so the police could go all the way up.

Sharpless and Karabell wheeled around to face the elevator, at the end of the room. With their eyes turned away, Nancy could risk moving. Ducking down, she crept behind a polished wooden food counter nearby. She slid stealthily closer to the two men and Sally.

With a whir of gears, the elevator doors rolled

open. Nancy saw Ned step out. As if it were happening in slow motion, she saw Evan Sharpless train his gun on Ned.

Then, moving surprisingly fast, Harold Karabell made a flying leap at Sharpless. He knocked the revolver out of Sharpless's hand and onto the floor.

Sharpless reeled backward from the blow. Still clutching Sally's arm, he crashed against the window behind him. Nancy gasped as she saw the glass shatter and break open.

Sharpless was falling out of the window—and Sally would go with him!

Chapter

Sixteen

SALLY CLAWED WILDLY at the window frame and held on for dear life. As Evan Sharpless pitched backward out the window, his hand slipped from her arm.

Then Sally did something Nancy would never forget. Twisting her body around, she grabbed Evan Sharpless's hand and she held on fiercely. Sharpless had threatened to kill her, and yet she was saving his life.

Then Harold Karabell dashed over and threw his arms around Sally's waist, so that the weight of Sharpless's body wouldn't pull her out the window. He, too, was helping to save the man who had double-crossed him.

Nancy and Ned arrived a second later, and they reached out to seize hold of the famous reporter's arms. Slowly, carefully, they hauled him back to safety.

A burst of applause broke out from the ground below. Nancy and Ned leaned over and looked down to see a crowd gathered on the ground far below, around the pair of police cars. Nancy thought she could see Bess and George there, too, waving enthusiastically up at them.

Nancy drew a deep breath and smiled at Ned. Just then, a half-dozen police officers stampeded up the fire stairs and circled Sharpless and Karabell. Hurrying in behind them, Maureen Peabody ran to Sally and put her arm around her shoulders.

Sally, shaking with relief, turned to Nancy. "Can we get out of here now?" she asked.

"Sorry, miss, but first we'll need to get a statement from you," a policeman said, snapping handcuffs onto Evan Sharpless's wrists. "And then I think you'd better give yourself a little rest. Sounds like you've been through a lot today."

Nancy reached over and squeezed Sally's hand. "I'll go to the banquet and tell Gina you're all right," she said, reading Sally's mind.

"Thanks, Nancy," Sally said with a grateful smile. "And one more thing. Can you find out if my photos won the competition?"

Nancy laughed. "After you so bravely exposed a fraud, how could anybody else possibly win?"

The buzz of young voices filled the banquet room as the student editors finished their last breakfast together. Nancy, George, and Bess paused on the threshold of the room. "I'll finally get to sit down in this room," Bess declared. "The food sure looks more tempting when you're going to eat it instead of serve it."

"Watch your backs!" Ned shouted from behind them. The three girls turned to see him wheeling a luggage trolley with a heavy bundle of newspapers.

"What's that, Nickerson?" Nancy asked.

"The morning edition of the *River Heights Record,*" Ned announced cheerfully. "Gina has ordered a copy for every student at the conference." He trundled on into the room, and the girls followed.

"Why is she being so generous all of a sudden?" George asked.

Parking the trolley, Ned broke the cords tying the bundle and lifted the top newspaper so they could see the front page. The main headline read, Network Newsman Arrested in Abduction of Student Photographer. And right below was the byline: Gina Fiorella.

Nancy gave a low whistle. "Gina had an article published in the paper?" she asked, impressed.

Ned nodded as he picked up a stack of papers. "Who else would know so much about the story already?" he said. "Didn't you notice how she pumped you for details, Nancy, when you returned to the banquet to tell her Sally was all right? As soon as you left, she ran out and called the editor, promising him an exclusive. You have to admit, the girl's got guts."

Gina came up behind Ned. Sally, still looking

worn out, tagged along behind her. "Has everybody seen my story, Ned dear?" Gina asked.

"I'm handing them out right now, Gina," he said. With a wink at Nancy and her friends, he stepped away to hand newspapers to students at the nearest table.

"Congratulations, Gina," Nancy said.

Gina shrugged and threw Nancy a dazzling smile. "Thanks. Quite a scoop, wasn't it?" she said, bragging. "They held the presses until I was finished writing, at three A.M. I ought to be exhausted, but I'm too excited to notice. And guess what?"

"What?" Nancy asked.

"The editor thought I did such a great job, he's offered me an internship on the paper next summer," Gina said. "So I guess you will all be seeing me next year. Isn't that great?"

Nancy could feel Bess poke her in the back. "Uh, yeah, great, Gina," Nancy stammered.

"I convinced the editor to give Sally an internship, too," Gina added, slipping an arm through her friend's elbow. "After all, it was her fantastic pictures that caught Sharpless in the act."

Sally smiled shyly. "It'll be fun to work on a daily paper," she said. "I'd much rather take pictures than be in the headlines myself."

Just then Jane Sellery walked by, a newspaper in her hand. "See my story on the front page, Jane?" Gina asked pointedly.

"Yeah," Jane said with a sneer. "Did you ask

your father to buy a new printing plant for the *Record?*" Jane flounced away, and Gina, scowling, trotted after her—to carry on their feud, Nancy thought.

Gary Ruxton walked up and joined the group. "Sally, I'm glad to see you back with us," he said. "You gave us quite a scare last night."

Sally rolled her eyes. "I certainly didn't mean to," she joked.

Mr. Ruxton smiled. "Well, I hope winning the photo contest helped to make up for your trouble. Congratulations. You deserved the prize."

"Thank you," Sally said, blushing modestly.

Mr. Ruxton turned to Nancy. "Any word on what Karabell and Sharpless will be charged with?"

"I chatted with the police after I gave them my statement last night," Nancy said. "They say Karabell will be charged with blackmail, but he may not ever be convicted. He claims he never asked Sharpless for hush money—Sharpless just offered it. Even though Karabell did take the money, he wasn't really extorting it."

"What about Sharpless?" Bess asked.

"Abduction, for one thing," Nancy began, counting off the charges on her fingers. "That's the most serious. Then unlawful entry, turning in a false fire alarm, two counts of arson, and three counts of reckless endangerment—for pushing the luggage trolley, for putting the dead rat on Gina's pasta, and for giving the oleander skewers

147

to the chef. And one charge of unlawful possession of a firearm."

"That's a lot of charges," Mr. Ruxton commented.

"He's confessed to everything, by the way," Nancy added. "The police officers I talked to assume he'll plead not guilty by reason of insanity. He might get off scot-free."

"That doesn't seem fair," Bess said.

Gary Ruxton tipped his head thoughtfully. "Whatever happens, Bess, his career is finished," he pointed out. "In a way, that's the harshest punishment of all for him."

Looking starry-eyed, Bess leaned toward the journalism teacher. "You have such insights into what makes a newsman tick," she said in a gushy voice.

Mr. Ruxton seemed baffled by her comment. "It's pretty basic human nature," he said. "Oh, by the way, Bess, I have a message for you, from one of the bellmen in the lobby. He asked me to tell you he'll be waiting to carry your bags when you check out this morning. I think he said his name was Ralph."

Bess's face crumpled. "Ralph?" she croaked.

"I think that was his name," Mr. Ruxton said. "He seems like a nice guy. Well, so long, girls, and thanks again for your help." With a friendly wave, he left.

"He probably thinks I'm *dating* Ralph," Bess said, and moaned. "The awful thing is, Ralph thinks so, too, just because I had a soda with him in the coffee shop the other day."

"You did?" George asked, incredulous.

"Well, I felt sorry for him!" Bess said, defending herself. "And besides, he's not *that* bad."

"Who's not that bad?" Paul Lampedusa asked, passing by with a coffee pot in his hand.

"Lampedusa, no socializing with the hotel guests," George said, a mischievous twinkle in her dark eyes. "Today I'm a hotel guest."

"I can't believe you were working undercover all that time," Paul declared. "You had me fooled."

"Oh, right, I was such a superb lifeguard, you really thought I was a pro," George said with a chuckle.

"We'll take this up later." Paul gave her a meaningful glance. He scooted over to a nearby table and got back to work.

Just then Bess glanced past Nancy to the door of the ballroom. "Look, there's Nick Kessler," she said, "still hanging around."

As the girls turned, they saw Gina wave and run over to her old bodyguard. "Oh, yeah," Sally said. "I forgot to tell you—Gina hired Nick back. When she found out that he'd stayed at the hotel for three days, still worried about her, she completely changed her mind about him. But she hasn't let Ned go yet. I don't think she's worked up the nerve."

Looking across the banquet room, Nancy

caught Ned's eye. He paused, a newspaper in his hand, and their gazes locked for a long, steady moment.

Nancy felt that old warm, tingly feeling flood through her. She turned back to Sally and said, "Somehow I don't think Ned will be too upset."

Nancy's next case:

Emerson College is jumping, and Nancy and George are ready to party. There's a major bash at Ned's fraternity and a gala art opening at the college museum. Michael Jared is one of America's hottest young artists—in more ways than one—and his new painting, *First Kiss,* has everyone talking. Especially the police . . . when it vanishes from the museum walls! The heist was a work of extraordinary agility and guile, and in conducting her investigation Nancy will have to be just as resourceful. Not only must she deal with a dangerously deceptive thief, she must also walk a tightrope of emotion. On the one side stands Ned, and on the other the charming and ever artful Michael Jared . . . in *The Stolen Kiss,* Case #111 in The Nancy Drew Files™.

THE HARDY BOYS CASEFILES